In The Moro

Joe Wise

Western Reflections, Inc.

Design by SJS Design (Susan Smilanic)

Antiques for cover supplied by Dick DePagter

Library of Congress Catalog Card Number: 99-61459

ISBN: 1-890437-24-7

Western Reflections, Inc.
P.O. Box 710, Ouray, Colorado 81427

For my parents who took me to the mountains.

ACKNOWLEDGMENT

Thanks to Patricia Joy Richmond for sharing with me her knowledge of the Fourth Expedition.

AUTHOR'S NOTE

Many of the events, people and places described in this book are based on fact. Some are fictitious.

Moro is a term used on the 1851 map by Bvt. 2nd Lt. John G. Parke, U.S.T.E. and Richard H. Kern to indicate a mountain range north of Santa Fe.

To my knowledge, there has never been a town of Moro.

It seems that when Col. Fremont returned from Taos, with the escort so kindly furnished by Major Beall, to the place where he had left his suffering companions, that HE FOUND THEM ALL DEAD! Not a living soul to tell the sufferings they had borne before their spirits took there final leave of all earthly affairs. It is natural to suppose what were the feelings of Col. Fremont and his party, at this sad – this trying spectacle. The number that died is supposed to be about thirty-eight. Col Fremont is himself very frosted and scarcely able to get about. In a few more, we hope to be able to state more particularly and in detail, the circumstances and facts connected with this affair, which must every where excite deep and absorbing interest.

Weekly Tribune (Liberty Missouri)
March 23, 1849

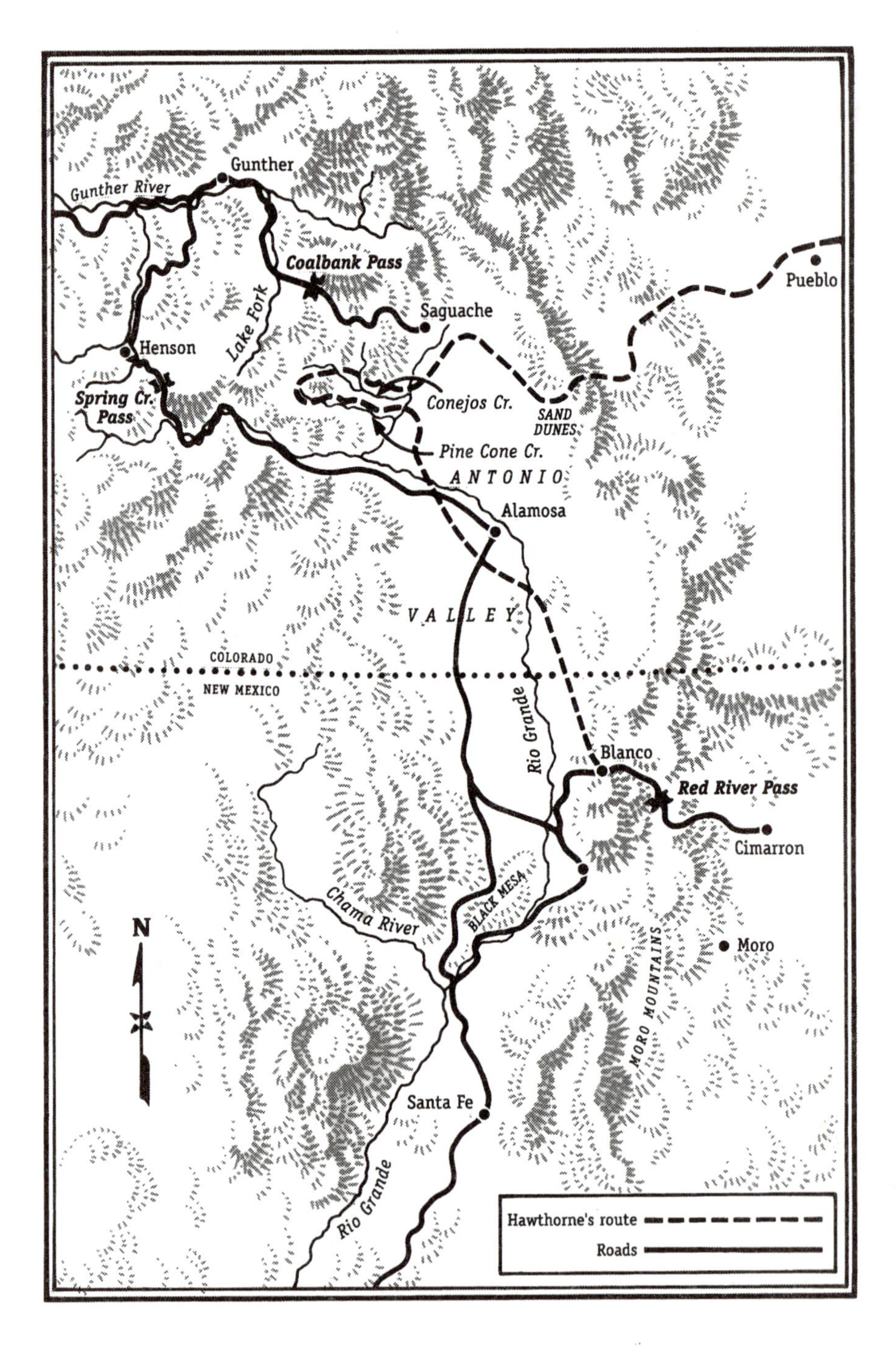
Gunther
Gunther River
Coalbank Pass
Pueblo
Saguache
Lake Fork
Henson
Spring Cr. Pass
Conejos Cr.
SAND DUNES
Pine Cone Cr.
ANTONIO
Alamosa
VALLEY
COLORADO
NEW MEXICO
Rio Grande
Blanco
Red River Pass
Cimarron
Chama River
BLACK MESA
Moro
MORO MOUNTAINS
N
Santa Fe
Rio Grande
Hawthorne's route
Roads

1

"From the looks of him, I'd say about three days. At least three days." The doctor had come up from Gunther when Sheriff Gibson called after finding Buster dead. Murders weren't common in Henson county. Mostly poachers, a rowdy drunk hassling his family, occasionally an abandoned car. But this was a murder for sure, and the sheriff needed a medical examiner.

"What makes you say that, Doc?"

"The rigor mortis is gone," the doctor said. "See here," he reached down and moved the dead man's arm to show that it was supple. "At this temperature it would take about three days for the stiffness to go. Between two and three days. And this color," he explained, pointing, "livor mortis it's called. It's all drained down to the back. "

Sheriff Gibson, as if to check on it, took the dead man's arm and pushed it away from him toward the wall, levering the body up on its right side. A mottled purple stain covered the dead man's back, his neck, even the back of his ears, like a giant birthmark.

The doctor bent slightly beside the sheriff to look. "It takes at least forty-eight hours to settle like that."

The bedsprings squeaked as the sheriff let the body roll back flat. A fist-sized hole had been blown in the dead man's chest, and the skin around the ragged, grey edges of the wound was peppered unevenly with dark macules the size of number six shot.

The two men stood looking at the body, the doctor making notes. "Twelve gauge most likely," the doctor said matter-of-factly,

writing. "Close range. No signs of a struggle. He must have been asleep. Asleep or drunk."

"Or both," the sheriff added. "Ol' Buster was drunk most of the time. He was asleep only part of the time."

The doctor was examining the dead man's hands. Without looking up he said, "Anything missing?" as if to give the sheriff something to do.

The sheriff turned and looked around the cluttered cabin. "How could you tell?"

The cabin where Buster had lived was made of rough-cut-logs, almost black with time, the color of creosote, chinked with cement and still papered, where they had not come off completely, with old newspapers. In the dry mountain air, newspapers could last, off-color and brittle, but readable for fifty years.

Originally the cabin had been the office for the ore mill at Cook's Falls, a hundred feet away. Nothing remained of the old mill except some broken stone foundations and scattered piles of coke and yellow rock.

Years ago Buster had just moved into the abandoned cabin. No one remembered exactly when, but he had lived there for so long that no one referred to it as Cook's Mill any longer. Everyone in town called it Buster's Cabin, except the children, who called it The Hermit's Cabin and were afraid to go there even to fish below the falls.

"Buster sure wasn't much of a housekeeper," the sheriff said, picking up a red and yellow chili can from the wood stove. The fluted can top had been turned back, a spoon still inside. The sheriff walked around the single room with the can in his hand.

The pipe of the rusted woodstove went out through a poor fit in the ceiling which was finished only on the front half, the other boards missing, or never placed. A Coleman lantern hung from a pulley near the center of the ceiling, suspended by a piece of clothesline rope that was tied to a nail in the wall near the dead man's bed.

In the middle of the room under the hanging lantern was a

small wooden table, a worn piece of red and white checkerboard oil cloth nailed to the top, and drawn up to it, a ladder-backed chair, the pressed cardboard bottom replaced with a piece of plywood nearly the right size. The sheriff dragged a finger across the dust on the top of the table and made a mental note.

The can still in his hand, the sheriff walked around the table to a single shelf nailed to the back wall near the stove. On it were several blue cans of vienna sausage, a cracker box, and some rags. From the wall behind the stove, a nearly naked "mechanic-ette" smiled coyly out into the cabin from Burdick's Auto Parts calendar.

"Nothing much to steal here," the sheriff said, turning back to the doctor who was still bent over the head of the bed closely inspecting the dead man's eyes. "Guess he just pissed somebody off. I'll come back later and take a few pictures. You'll need some help with the body?"

"Un-huh," the doctor said straightening up. He wrote something on a tablet, looked for a few seconds at what he had written, then folded the top of the tablet and put it in his shirt pocket. "No family, I suppose?"

"Maybe over at Moro. I never saw anyone with him as a rule. He was pretty much a loner."

"What's his last name?" the doctor asked.

"Dickey was the name he used when Buster wasn't enough. Buster Dickey."

"What do you mean the name he used?" the doctor asked, confused.

"His real name was Cordova," the sheriff said.

"Same as the Cordovas in Moro?"

"Yep, but I don't think he wanted anyone around here to know that."

The doctor frowned. "How come?"

"People around here don't think much of the Cordovas. Pretty rough bunch."

"Why don't we drive over to Moro tomorrow and ask around?"

the doctor suggested.

"Fine with me, but don't expect much help."

"You mean on account of your being a sheriff?"

"I mean on account of our being Anglos."

2

It took a little more than twenty minutes for the slip of sunlight to move across the contours of the pillow. When the bright rectangle lit David Walton's face, the warmth waked him. For a few seconds he was confused. He didn't recognize the room. Log beams ran across the ceiling. His consciousness slowly cleared. Logs. Log cabin. Colorado. Henson, Colorado.

David stretched, put his hands behind his head and looked over at the clock. He had napped for two hours. Before his retirement, he had rarely had time for a nap. He swung his feet from the bed, sat for a minute feeling rather fortunate, then got up and walked out into the kitchen. He took a can of beer from the refrigerator and went outside to survey his new world.

The cabin he had bought was in an aspen grove, on a dry, grassy slope overlooking the river and the narrowing upper valley to the south. Two old ponderosa pines, their trunks striped orange and black, grew at the corner of the porch. Mountains rose abruptly behind the cabin, and just across the river, making the little valley around him feel close and private. From where he stood, no other cabins were in sight, and there was no sound except the steady, liquid machinery of the river.

He sat down on the grass and leaned back against the log wall that had been warmed by the afternoon sun. The fall air was delicious. The sky was huge and clear. Green-backed swallows, acrobats, wheeled and darted over the river.

David had always felt at home in these mountains. Even when he had come here in the vacation summers of his childhood. From the beginning everything had seemed immediately familiar, a

comfortable satisfaction that had grown with each trip back to Henson. Later he would tell only his closest friends he had become convinced that he had lived another life, and that this mountain valley was where he had lived and maybe even died.

After he was grown David had brought his own family here, and after his children were older, he had returned almost every summer, sometimes with his wife Susan and sometimes with his brother. Sometimes he came alone.

For him, the mountains had always seemed overpowering. Gladiators, rulers, patriarches, yet so confidently quiet. Their commanding size seemed to call for shouts rather than silence. Full orchestras, and triumphant, dominant major chords. And yet, except for an occasional Wagnerian show of force, the music of the mountains was peaceful, restful, a still, dominant calm – quiet enough to hear the lilt and twinkle of birdsong, the wind in the trees, the pleasant staccato of the streams.

So far his retirement had gone very well. After twenty-five years of being on call as a physician, David found it particularly pleasant to be the master of his own time. He fished when he wanted. He spent the day out with his camera, waiting for the perfect light, waiting for the clouds to move. Someday he would finish the darkroom. He took naps when he wanted. No one called to ask his advice, or make an appointment, or request his presence at a meeting. He had a telephone, but it never rang. So far he was not lonely.

He wrote letters, read, and went to town for mail and groceries and gasoline. Occasionally he bought a paper. He had no television. There was no unwanted stimulation, only that which he sought out. At that moment, as he sat against the warmth of the wall, the only decision he had to make was what he would have for supper.

As he sat looking up the valley, the sun slowly moved behind Crystal Peak, and the shadows began to claim the west side of his view, from the top down. In an hour it would be dark. He would build a fire and have supper and then work on his paper.

He had just finished supper when Dub drove up. David met him at the door.

"By golly, it's good to see you, Doc!" said the old man, getting out of his pickup. "Welcome back." He shook David's hand with both of his. "You're looking good." Dub Ponder was seventy years old. He never seemed to change. Same plaid flannel shirt. Same Levi's. Same cigar. He looked like a leprechaun. His eyes twinkled when he talked and when he laughed, which was often, they disappeared completely. Dub ran the dude ranch in Henson where David and his family had spent their vacations.

"Come on in," David said. "Sit down. Sit down," guiding Dub to the kitchen table.

"By golly, it's good to see you," Dub said again as he was sitting down. "You haven't been up in awhile. How's your brother?" Dub always asked about David's brother when he saw him, and always asked about David when he saw Harry. "He still live in Ft. Worth?"

"San Antonio."

"San Antonio. That's right." Dub was smiling. His front teeth, top and bottom, were worn down to small pegs. Sand in the cigar wrappers did that. "Your brother and his boys were up last summer," Dub continued. "They camped up Acme Creek canyon. Didn't stay with us, but he stopped by the house to say hello." Then he said it again," By golly, Doc, it's good to see you."

"I'm sorry I missed you when I came in last month," David said. "Jolene said you were off in Denver politicking."

"Finally got the deed to our place here," he said with a 'you-wouldn't-believe-it' tone, "It's all legal now. Twenty-five years fighting with those bureaucrats. Senator Pitkin helped us with it. Four trips to Washington. Three lawyers. What a go around! But she's all set now." He rolled the cigar with his tongue from the right side of his mouth to the left side. From the looks of it, the cigar had been out for hours. David knew what was coming next.

"Dad settled the place, you know," Dub continued. "He rode over from Gunther in 1888. The old ranch was up on the hill where the summer pasture is. One winter right before the war we brought the old house down the hill to the road where it is now. What a trip. Brought 'er down on skids. Broke out every windowpane."

"That's where it was when I first came," David reminded him. "Why did you move it?"

"Well, I wanted it down nearer the road so the tourists could see it. But I wanted a good view. I took an old window frame and walked around looking through it 'til I found a view I liked, and I put the house right there."

David laughed.

"You know," said Dub, the cigar shifted," I remember that night when you and your folks first came here. Musta' been in 1942. During the war. We didn't get off to a very good start," he laughed. "Your dad drove up to the house just after dark and asked for a cabin, but we were full. At that time we only had four cabins. I told him to come back at 9:30 and we'd have one. After he drove off I got Jolene and the kids, and we worked for two hours cleaning out that old cabin across the road. We'd been using it for a chicken house, but what the heck, two dollars was two dollars." Cigar back to the left.

"When your folks came back, I took them over to look at it. Your momma took one look and said, 'I'm not staying in that place!'" Dub laughed.

David had heard this story before. It was one of Dub's favorites.

"She told me she saw a rat run across the floor just as she walked in," David said.

"Coulda' been. Coulda' been," Dub laughed. "Anyway you all took off. I don't remember where you went. You know I never did get that two dollars."

"We moved in with some friends from home who were staying at Mrs. Fisk's," David said. "Must have been several years before we started staying at your place."

"Well, I'm glad you did. I watched you boys grow up."

"It's a great place."

"It's 'God's country,' Doc." Dub smiled to himself at the thought of it. "Say, Doc," Dub said, looking around the cabin, "Jolene says you've bought this place."

"I'm moving here. I retired."

"Retired," Dub said surprised. "You're not old enough to retire. Where's the...?"

"The wife?"

"Yeah."

"She died, Dub"

"Oh, God, Doc. I'm sorry to hear that. What in the world happened?"

"She was killed in a car accident. Three years ago."

"Oh, no! And she was so pretty."

"Yeah, what a waste. The kids really had a hard time. They were all so close." David didn't tell Dub that he had been utterly, completely, devastated, that he didn't work for a year and that even now found himself thinking of things he wanted to tell her or show her. But there wasn't anyone he could tell yet. "Made it kind of hard to come here, actually. She liked it here a lot."

"Golly Doc, that's terrible. Jolene will hate to hear this."

"Well, I know. It's bad. We had talked about retiring here someday. We had even looked at that place across from Cloudcroft Ranch when it was for sale a few years ago, the forest ranger's place, but we were worried about the price. When we came back the next year it had sold, so we just chalked it up to fate. Should have bought it."

"What about your kids?"

"They're both still in college. They seem to be doing okay now, but the accident was pretty tough on them for awhile. I'm just glad for them that they weren't younger. It was bad enough as it was."

Dub shook his head slowly as David talked. "How're you holdin' out, Doc?"

"I'm doing okay," David lied.

Uncomfortable, Dub changed the subject. "Well...what about the practice back in New Jersey?"

"New Hampshire," David corrected him. "Well, I just told my partners I wanted out. They understood. I gave them a year to find a new partner, then I took off. I sold the house in New Hampshire and lived in Texas for awhile."

"You grew up in Fort Worth, didn't you?"

"Yes, but it has changed a lot. It's a big city now, and it's still hot. After I came back to Texas I thought a lot about Henson. I never could have lived here when I was practicing. I considered coming up here and opening an office, but it's too small for a cardiologist, and I have forgotten all the general medicine I ever knew. Besides, I'd have to be on call every day. I had always wondered,

though, what it would be like to live here year 'round. The summers were wonderful, but I thought it would be good to see all the seasons. So, when I retired I thought, hey, why not now? I remembered reading about that guy who was walking across the country and stopped here to spend the winter and work on his book. I was always a little jealous of him."

"Nice young fellow," Dub said, relieved to be talking about something else. "He stayed in one of our cabins, Number four, that whole winter. He put me in his book you know," Dub said proudly. "He put my picture in it too. I've got a copy of the book at the house. He signed it."

David knew that. He had a copy of the book, too. Reading it had started him thinking about retiring in Henson.

"So you're not going to do any doctoring here?"

"Nope. I'm all finished with that. Twenty-five years is enough. Time to slow down and do some of the things I have wanted to do before I get too old and crippled."

"Old and crippled!" Dub laughed. "I suspect it will be awhile before you are old and crippled! You couldn't be much over, what, forty-five?"

"Fifty-three," David said.

"Boy, don't I wish I was fifty-three." Dub leaned back, remembering. "Doc, you know what I was doing when I was fifty-three? I was bulldozing a road for that oil company up on the backside of Iron Mountain. You can still see it from Alpine Creek. Took all summer. We never even came down at night. Slept up there. You talk about some pretty spot. They were looking for uranium. We go up there in elk season now, but that's different from working on a bulldozer." Dub shifted the cigar again. "Fifty-three. Boy-oh-boy, wouldn't I like to be fifty-three."

"Say, Dub." Dub's eyebrows rose in a "What?" "There's something I have been wanting to ask you."

"What's that?" Dub said, eager to be helpful.

"Have you ever heard anything about an expedition led by a man named Hawthorne that came through here somewhere in the 1840s? They were looking for a route through the mountains for the railroad."

"Some," Dub said, leaning forward on his elbows, concentrating. "Why?"

"Well, I got interested in it a few years ago when I learned they might have come through somewhere near here."

"They all died," said Dub. "I know that. Just like Packwood's bunch." In 1874, a prospector named Alfie Packwood had killed and eaten his five mining partners during a severe winter that had trapped them in the Henson valley. It was everyone's favorite story in Henson.

"Hawthorne and the guide made it out."

"Yep. Just like Packwood".

"I was wondering if they might have tried to cross anywhere near Spring Creek Pass. No one really knows exactly where they were when they got lost."

"Well," Dub said, thinking, "there are some tree stumps over on Varden Peak that are cut off as much as sixteen feet above the ground. Two or three bunches of them. Cut off high like they would have been if they were cut in deep snow. I was over there once and I couldn't reach the tops of the tallest stumps from horseback. No one knows for sure who cut them. Maybe it was Hawthorne's bunch. Frank Simpson, the forest ranger, always said it was explorers who did it, but there were a lot of mines in that area and the miners might have cut them."

"I thought the miners pretty well cleared out in the winter."

"Most of them did," Dub agreed, "and Simpson always said that's one of the things that made him think the explorers cut them."

"One of the things?" David encouraged. "What else?"

"The trees looked like they were cut down by people who didn't know much about cutting trees."

"What do you mean?"

"They look like they were cut down with hatchets," Dub said, gesturing. "Short, hacking chops. Upward swings. Not the big bites of an ax."

"Are the stumps still there?" David asked.

"I don't know," said Dub. "Maybe. Wood doesn't rot very quickly at that altitude, you know. It musta' been twenty years since I was up there. Maybe more. They were there then. Never had a reason

to go back. No elk, and in the summer the lightning would keep you away. Maybe they are still there. Some of them had fallen down then, but others were easy to see. And they did look kinda' like campsites," he added.

"Campsites?"

"Well, Simpson pointed it out to me. There were three or four groups of them. All pretty much the same. They were in the kind of places you would make an elk camp. Right at the timberline in a group of trees for shelter, on the west bank of a stream so you would have first light. I suppose it could be true."

"Where is Simpson now?"

"He's been dead quite awhile. Matter-of-fact, he was transferred out of this area. I think to Wyoming. Or Montana. I heard he died out there. Never married that I know of."

"Can you take me up to Varden Peak sometime? I'd like to look around."

"You bet," Dub said with a nod. "We'll need horses. It'll take all day to get up and back. But we ought to wait 'til next month, unless you're in a big hurry."

"Why?"

"Thunderstorms will be pretty much over by then. You sure don't want to be up there in one o' them, I can tell you for sure. I've been up high in a thunderstorm, and I can tell you that's something you wouldn't want to do on purpose. Lightning striking every ten feet. Thunder almost continuous and loud enough to make you wet your pants. Too much variety for me." As he talked, he stretched back in his chair straightening his legs, leaning first to the right, then to the left, searching his pants pockets the best he could without standing. Finally he retrieved a Zippo lighter and lit the stump of his cigar, rolling it in the flame to make sure it was lit all around.

"You know anything about animal bones Doc?" Dub asked, puffing.

"Not much, why?"

"There were bones all over up there that Simpson said were mule bones. He said they belonged to the explorers. He said there were lots of them, but I only saw a few. Maybe there are some left."

"Mule bones?"

"They looked like horse bones to me." He blew smoke at the ceiling. "But I couldn't figure horses at that altitude. Not that many of 'em, at any rate. Miners used some jacks, but the bones he showed me looked too big to be jacks. Maybe you could tell, if there are any of them left."

"It would be easy enough to find somebody who could," David said. "Hawthorne had fifty mules with him on the trip. All of them died."

"Fifty mules would leave a lot of bones, all right. They might be the bones."

David was excited to think that he might have already found some new information related to the Hawthorne route. "If those stumps mark the Hawthorne campsites, we have really discovered something. Varden Peak could be the snowy ridge that they thought was the Continental Divide. "

"It's not the Divide, though," Dub corrected.

"I know, but they were probably lost. No one with them had ever been in those mountains before, except maybe the guide, but that's not for sure."

"I guess I never knew all that much about the Hawthorne Expedition," Dub admitted. "What got you so interested in that, anyway?"

"Well, it's a mystery," David said. "I like historical mysteries."

"Golly, Doc!" Dub said suddenly, looking at his watch. "Jolene's gonna kill me! I was supposed to be getting paper towels. 'Gotta' go!" He stood up from behind the table and walked stiffly to the door. David got up with him and followed him out. "Doc, you've got to come up and have supper with us," Dub said as he walked. Dub's ranch was just up the river from David's cabin. "You shouldn't spend your time alone here." Dub was very gregarious, and it was hard for him to understand how David could enjoy being alone.

"I was hoping you would ask," David joked. "I would love it." He walked with Dub over to his pickup and stood by the side as Dub got in and closed the door.

"By golly," he said through the open window," it's good to see you, Doc. I'm glad you're back. Stop up and let's talk some more."

"You bet."

Dub started the truck and, with a wave, drove off. David watched him drive off. Then he went back into the house, took the map tubes out of the closet, and unrolled the maps on the kitchen table. It was midnight before he went to sleep.

I have never known such cold, nor seen the snow so deep upon the mountains. It has been snowing steadily for four days and during that time the mercury has not risen from of the bulb of the thermometer. Even at this hour there is no sign of let up.

Yesterday we came with considerable difficulty over a high barren ridge and made it only a mile to this place. The snow, even on the ridge was in places shoulder deep and, driven by the wind into a pouderie, was so thick in the air that we could not see five yards ahead. With shovels and mauls we attempted to beat a trail through the snow, but the winds drifted it full before the main party could follow. The mules, weakened after so many days without food, floundered in the deep snow. Some fell down dead. Others fell, and unable to rise under their burdens, had to be helped to their feet. Much time was consumed unpacking and repacking the poor creatures and the effort further drained the men's failing strength.

After seven hours of strenuous labor we were able to cross the ridge and descend a short way down into the tree line, where completely exhausted, we made what camp we could. Had we been one half hour more on the ridge we would have all surely frozen. We are camped now in a small grove of trees just below the ridge top. The altimeter indicates 12,000 feet above sea level, but in this cold I am not sure that it is correct. Even in the trees the snow driven by the relentless wind has drifted too deep to stand. The men, wrapped in what blankets they have not made shoes of, are huddled together in separate messes of six or eight, only their bowed heads showing above the edge of the deep pits which their fires have already melted in the snow. Beyond the black of the trees in every direction all is white and it is impossible to distinguish the ground from the sky. Godfrey led the mules to the top of the next ridge to what appeared to be a grassy area blown free of snow. He struggled for two hours to reach it only to find that what appeared to be grass was not grass at all but the tops of buckbrush six feet high protruding from the

snow. He was forced by the wind and the cold to leave the mules behind, fruitlessly pawing at the deep snow, and he himself barely made it back to the trees. I doubt any of the mules will survive the night. They have already eaten some of the tug ropes and the strapping on the pack saddles and even each other's manes and tails and as I write this I can hear between the violent blasts of the wind the plaintive braying of these helpless creatures. Just after we arrived at this place, I sent Walker out to reconnoiter a possible route for the next day. I watched him go out against the winddriven snow which obscured my sight of him before he had gone fifty yards. He returned in an hour, senseless and nearly frozen. Icicles hung from his moustache and even his eyelashes, and his hair and his blanket and his clothes were frozen together in a solid mass. As he fell beside me, blood started from his nose and froze on his cheek. He was half an hour by the fire before he could speak. He said the divide, which we thought we had already crossed, was still ahead, perhaps two days away, but beyond that the descent into the Coalbank Pass was gradual. The old man tried to appear confident, but I fear that he is lost and a terrible despair has come over me.

Tonight I was too exhausted to eat, but forced myself to take some broth made from mule meat. The snow and the wind continue unabated. I have, on none of my journeys, been so cold. The fire partly warms only the side turned towards it, the other side being covered with drifting snow, and it is necessary to turn frequently. The sooty pine smoke is blinding, but away from the fire, the cold is unbearable. Sleep is impossible. The men who have followed so bravely and so long are failing now. I can see that they are exhausted and in danger of freezing. Their spirit is waning with their strength. I saw it in their eyes for the first time today, their high hopes of October turned to despair. Old Walton is still sick and we do the best we can to comfort him. Tonight, the last of the mules will surely die. Without them, we can not go on. We have been overtaken by ruin. I have no hope of continuing now. The unthinkable has become the inevitable. We must – and I can scarcely bring myself to write the words - turn back - and make for the safety of the river. I feel as if I have lost control. Yesterday I thought we might succeed. Tonight I pray, with luck, we might survive.

3

For David Walton, it had been a fifteen-year hobby, musing about the disastrous mountain expedition and how it had gone wrong. Even though it had been more than a hundred years ago, the mysteries surrounding the expedition had a compelling currency about them that had fascinated David, and he found trying to solve them irresistible.

What would drive men to set out on foot to cross the Rocky Mountains in the winter? Why, considering the importance of an experienced guide on such an adventure, would the expedition have left St. Louis without one? And why, after finally taking on a guide, would the leader of the expedition ignore his advice and turn the party away from the trail that might have led to safety and success to one that led to death and disaster?

The leader of the expedition, James Hawthorne, had been a fortunate man, at least before the mountain tragedy. The son of a wealthy ship line owner, Hawthorne had grown up in comfortable East Coast prosperity. It was a world of tutors and travel, of riding instructors and shooting weekends, of music and art and important house guests.

At eighteen, he had been accepted into the prestigious Hampden Military Academy, where as expected, he excelled at mathematics, astronomy, and leadership. After graduating, at the urging and by the arrangement of his father, young James went on his first western adventure, an expedition led by the French cartographer Jaques Millet, to map the upper Missouri.

On that trip Hawthorne fell in love with the West and he wrote home of his new excitement with the freedom of the wilderness, the vastness of the open space and the plains, the mountain ranges and unbridged rivers.

From Millet, Hawthorne learned not only a respect and fascination for the unknown, but also the the value of order and precision, the logistics of organizing and managing an expedition, the tactics of dealing with and overcoming adversity and inconvenience, and even danger – skills that would eventually make him the pathfinder for his generation.

The Missouri Expedition had been a widely publicized success. Territories were mapped, fort sites were plotted, rivers were traced to their origins, trading treaties with the Indians were secured. Overnight Hawthorne had become a credible explorer. He left home a student and returned a hero. He was now a protegé of Millet's and he shared in his fame.

When Millet made the report of his expedition to Congress, Hawthorne was at his side. Hawthorne attended the official celebrations, he was invited to state dinners and balls, and at the age of twenty-three he was awarded a lieutenant's commission in the newly formed United States Corps of Topographical Engineers. Successful, dashing, bright, and now famous, he had already become everything that most men his age could only dream of. On his twenty-fourth birthday, he married Rebecca Mansell, the daughter of the United States ambassador to France.

For twenty years, James Munroe Hawthorne did more to make the West known than perhaps any other single individual. Favored by time and circumstance, he was an explorer-scientist, an adventurer blazing new trails, using modern instruments to make the first accurate maps and reporting his adventures in sensational narratives which stirred the imagination of a restless nation and made the concept of Manifest Destiny irresistible.

Energetic, capable, vain and ambitious, he became a national hero. Before his remarkable career was over, he would circumnavigate the West, serve in the United States Senate, and except for the electoral votes of Pennsylvania, would have been the nation's sixteenth president.

James Hawthorne's only bad year was 1849. In the fall of that year just before beginning his presidential campaign, he and a company of thirty-three men set out to cross the Rocky Mountains in the first attempt to survey a central route for the railroad to the Pacific. Two weeks before he left his infant son died. Perhaps it was an omen. But, as if driven, he continued across the plains and into the mountains where, lost and trapped by severe winter weather, all except Hawthorne and his guide died. Almost immediately the controversy began.

Questions were raised about Hawthorne's leadership, about his resolve, his judgment. Perhaps Hawthorne was too desperate for success. Perhaps, out of pride, Hawthorne insisted on the wrong route, or stubbornly pushed on even after all hope of success was gone. Perhaps Hawthorne's selection of guides was unfortunate, or unschooled. Perhaps the expedition was doomed from the start. The route was strenuous and the weather was severe beyond imagination. Perhaps no matter who the leader, was the mountains and the winter would have won.

Although David's interest in Hawthorne's Expedition was long-lived, it had begun as an accident. Chance. Serendipity. He was led to it by a series of events only partially related.

He had seen the reference to Hawthorne's expedition while he was researching another disastrous mountain adventure. Not a momentous continental crossing, not a reputation-building junket, not a conquest that could affect the politics and fortune of a nation. The adventure that first caught David's imagination was not the single misfortune of a leader with one piece of bad luck, but the desperate trials of a loser with no luck at all.

"There's the Packwood Massacre site, boys," David's father would say every year as they drove past the six white posts set in a rectangle and linked with painted chains. It wasn't necessary for him to point it out. David would have already seen it. He would have been watching for it from the moment they started down off the pass into the little mountain valley

where they spent their vacations. David knew exactly where to look and it was easy to see the white posts on the bluff overlooking the river, and he knew that buried there were the remains of the bodies of the five men Alfie Packwood had eaten.

Like all boys who had ever come to Henson, David had been fascinated by the gruesome story of murder and cannibalism. The Packwood Massacre was the local legend in Henson, the little mountain town, where for twenty years, David's father had brought his family on vacation. The drug store in Henson sold pamphlets recounting the story of the "San Juan Cannibal". In the postcard rack beside the cash register, among the fishing scenes and mountain views, were photographs of Alfie Packwood and the grave sites for the non-believers.

David had been hypnotized by the pictures of the secluded campsite where the men's bodies had been found lying face up within a few feet of each other, their butchered corpses, almost skeletons, still partly covered with the ragged remnants of their clothes, their feet still bandaged in the strips of blanket that, in the end, had served for shoes. From the death mask faces, twisted in agony, it was clear that something horrible had happened there.

Drawn by a naive and compelling child's curiosity, David had often gone to the grave site, the fenced slab bearing the names of the five men. He tried to visualize them in their last desperate days, tried to imagine their terror, their fears, and their faces. There behind the safety and security of the skirts and petticoats of time, he felt a sort of guilty thrill as he looked on the scene of violence he could only imagine.

The Massacre, as it was called in Henson, had taken place in 1874. That winter five goldseekers had hired Alfie Packwood, a penniless drifter, to lead them through the San Juan Mountains to a new gold strike at Breckenridge. The six men had left Salt Lake City in November, and after two months, arrived at the junction of the Gunther and the Uncompahgre rivers, the site of a Ute Indian winter camp. The men were welcomed into the camp and advised by the Indians to remain until spring, that attempting to cross the mountains was very dangerous because of the snow and the cold.

The men stayed at the Indian camp for three weeks, but then unable to control the restless impatience of their gold fever any longer, they left the camp with ten days' rations and headed for the Los Alamos Indian Agency seventy-five miles away. Two months later Packwood, bearded and exhausted, stumbled into the agency alone.

He told the men at the Indian Agency a horrible tale of weakness and prostration, of paralytic cold and deep imprisoning snow, of futile hunts for food, of starvation and fear.

He said that shortly after the the six men had left the Indian camp, their supplies had run out. Blinded by a snowstorm, they wandered for four days, until terrified and faint with hunger, they realized that they were lost. On the sixth day, Thomas Noonan,the oldest of the group, sick and weak from the ordeal, died. Crazed with hunger the men ate his body. But almost immediately the relentless starvation returned, and with it, the new fear that made sleep impossible.

Packwood told how, returning to camp one day from an unsuccessful hunt for game, he had found Shannon Hoskiss alone by the fire. Surprised, Hoskiss tried to kill him, but Packwood shot him with his rifle. Later he said, he had found the bodies of the other four men, one partially eaten, their skulls split open with an axe.

Immediately the men at the Agency began a search for the bodies, but none was found until five months later when they were accidently discovered by miners prospecting in the area. Packwood was arrested.

Impatience Packwood said, had caused the party to leave the Indian camp where they should have waited out the winter to hurry to the gold fields. Bad luck had brought the white-out blizzard that lasted four days. Fate turned them up the wrong canyon where they tried to fend off starvation eating rose hips and finally their moccasins.

Packwood, who probably was not a guide at all, and may never have been in the San Juans before, did admit that he had lived off the bodies of the dead companions, but that, he said, was no more than anyone would have done under the circumstances. Convicted of murder and cannibalism, Packwood died in prison.

As David had outgrown his youthful preoccupation with the details of deceit and violence, he had become more interested in exactly how Packwood's party came to where it had floundered. How had they come to this little valley so far off the route to Breckenridge? Had Packwood taken them there to rob them? Had Packwood really taken the wrong turn, as he said, and if so, what trail did he turn from? What trail did he turn to? Had they come in from the south, over what was later Badger Pass? If so, why did they stop where they did? Did they come up the valley from the north, make a wrong turn, following the trap of the valley?

The trails fascinated David. "Mountain trails were not made," he had written in his juvenile journal, "they were discovered. They existed from the time of the mountains themselves, secret, creased rewards found first by the water and then the walkers. In the mountains, it was the trails that directed the travelers and determined the history. Trails led up the tributary streams, always part-way up on the ridge, above the boulders and the brush in the water courses, to high saddle ridges, crossing only at passes, then, mirror-imaged down. Trails and passes were not random. They had names. They were natural things."

Searching for trails in the Henson area that Packwood might have taken, David had sought out old maps, "drawings of their memory." But, on the few that he could find, the wilderness around the Henson valley was inked in with artful, stylized little mountain ranges and ridges. Large unnamed areas were blank except for the curved notations, *Spur of the Main Range or Sage Plain*. On most of the maps, even the river and stream drainages, if they were drawn in, were wrong.

One map at the Huntington Library had shown a dotted trail the lost party should have followed, but it was far to the north of the massacre site, a nameless track along the river leading from the area of the Indian winter camp to the wide valley and the Breckenridge road, a trail that the party had turned from - lost or lured - one valley too soon.

Then, by chance, while he was looking in a copy of *Mountain Gates and Passes* for trail maps of the Henson area, David had seen the reference. Walker's Pass. It was a pass he had never heard of. The exact location was not given. The index had no other listing for Walker's Pass, but just below it, in bold print, was the entry that had stunned him. "**Walton, M., 315.**" David had written to his brother:

"This is too mystical! You know how I have always had the feeling that I had lived in Henson before? Well, a Matthew Walton was with James Hawthorne when he tried to get through the mountains somewhere near Henson in the winter of 1848 looking for a railroad route to the Pacific. Matthew Walton died there – that seems strange to say. He froze, the first of the thirty-three to die, at what Hawthorne called Christmas Camp, wherever that is. Matthew Walton was from St. Louis, but I haven't been able to find out much about him or where he came from. Everyone was from St Louis in those days. Matthew is a common Walton family name. I'll bet he was a relative! Probably went to St. Louis from Georgia. I've got to read more about the Hawthorne Expedition. You wouldn't believe what those guys went through before they died. I'm sending you copies of one of the diaries."

It had been fifteen years since David had written that letter. During that time many things about his life had changed. But he had never lost interest in Hawthorne's expedition. He could never completely give up on the idea that he might be the one who would somehow solve the riddle of it.

Although his medical practice didn't leave him much spare time, he continued, when he could, to work on the Project, as he called it. He read what little he could find about the expedition and the men involved. He reviewed his notes and maps looking for clues he might have missed. Occasionally he wrote to someone he thought might have a new lead. But still, there were too many missing pieces, too many dead ends, and the same questions continued to tease him, popping up to trouble him when he least expected it, while he shaved, or as he drove to work or at night, just before he slept.

4

The Pine Cone Cafe was the only place in Henson to get cooked food after dark. Actually, it was a bar, but there was a small kitchen in the back beyond the booths and the pool table and the Olympia beer light.

David had come for the enchiladas, partly because he had heard they were good, partly because he didn't want to cook, and partly just to see the Pine Cone again. It had been called the Log Cabin when he was there last, but only the name had changed since the first time he had sneaked in as a teenager to play pool.

The old wooden bar, ornate and nearly black, ran along the left wall near the front door. David took a stool and looked around. The only other person in the place was an old man in a khaki down vest sitting at the other end of the bar. Leaning forward, his hand cupped to his ear, trying to watch an old war movie on the television, he hadn't looked up when David came in.

Behind the bar under a large elk head was a long mirror, and under the mirror a dark counter top lined with liquor bottles and their reflections. Someone had put sunglasses on the elk. On the other side of the room, across from the bar, was a small raised platform, most of it covered by an old upright piano, leaving barely enough room for three folding chairs.

A young woman wearing Levi's and a Sea World sweatshirt came out of the kitchen, walked the length of the room, and turned in behind the bar between the man and the television war. She put a napkin down on the bar in front of David and looked at him expectantly. "Hello," she said. "What'll it be?"

"Can I eat here at the bar, or should I sit at a table?" David asked.

"With this crowd?" she laughed, motioning to the empty room. "You're fine." She wasn't the bartender he had expected.

"Do you have enchiladas tonight?"

"Every night," she said, flipping a towel over her shoulder.

"That's what I'm having. And a Coors," David added. "Or make that Olympia," he corrected himself as she turned to the refrigerator. He had never been able to decide whether he liked Coors or Olympia better. Probably they were the same.

She put the beer can on the napkin. "Red or green?" she asked.

David looked puzzled.

"Do you want red or green chili on your enchiladas?"

"Red," David said. He had forgotten that he had a choice. In Texas there was only red.

"Three minutes," she said. She walked back through the long room and out the door into the kitchen.

David was looking forward to the enchiladas, but actually he had come to the Pine Cone hoping to meet Jack Fuller. He had tried to find Fuller's number in the Gunther phone book, but there was no listing. A call to the college hadn't helped much. Yes, Jack Fuller had taught there, the girl who answered had said, but not for the past three years. He had moved, but she didn't know exactly where. She thought maybe Henson. The postmistress in Henson confirmed that a Jack Fuller received mail, general delivery, but she wouldn't tell David if there was any mail in the box.

David had bought a post card and addressed it to "Jack Fuller, General Delivery, Henson, Colorado." On it he explained briefly who he was, that he wanted to talk about Hawthorne, and that he could be reached at 942-1636. Two weeks went by without a call, unless he had missed it.

Dub hadn't known of any professor, and that made it unlikely

that Fuller was living in Henson, but he suggested trying the Pine Cone. "Most everyone goes there sooner or later," he said.

Jack Fuller had written the best piece on Hawthorne. The Colorado Historical Society had published it as a separate booklet. A lot of what David had learned about the expedition was from that booklet, but it hadn't dealt much with the expedition's actual route. David hadn't seen anything written by him since. Looking up Fuller was one of the things David had hoped to have time for, but never had, until now. Fuller wasn't at the college in Gunther, as David had hoped, but if he was in Henson it would be even better.

The war at the other end of the bar ended. The TV man strained slowly over the bar and snapped off the power. He sat back heavily, took a cigarette deliberately from a package on the bar, and with some difficulty, lit it with a match, turning his face up and away from the flame, squinting his left eye. Several slow waves put out the match, and as if summoned, the bartender-waitress appeared with David's enchiladas.

"Hot plate," she warned David as she slid the oblong white platter down on the bar in front of him.

On a scale of 1-10, the enchiladas were maybe an upper seven. The cheese was no good. It was always the cheese. Too rubbery. The best was half Monterey Jack and half Velveeta. David was convinced that's what the best Mexican food places used, but no one would ever admit it. Before David had finished, the TV man turned slowly off his stool and walked toward the door.

"Night, Claude," the bartender said as the old man passed. Claude waved indifferently without looking back, and walked out.

She watched him go, smiling kindly.

After she said, "How are the enchiladas?" and he said, "Fine," David said, "Do you know a man named Jack Fuller?"

She looked surprised. "He's my neighbor." Then thinking it over, she added, "Well, not exactly my neighbor. Why? Do you know him?"

"No, but I know of him. He wrote a book," David said, explaining. "A history book. I would like to talk to him about it, but I haven't been able to find him. I called the college in Gunther where he taught, but he's no longer there. The woman I talked to at the college said she thought he might be living around here."

The bartender seemed a little hesitant.

"You know where I might find him or how I can get in touch with him?" David said carefully.

"He's probably at home."

"Does he live here in Henson?"

"Not exactly."

"I tried sending him a card here in Henson," David said, "general delivery, but so far no answer. Do you know if he is home? Maybe I could call him?"

"What's your name?"

"Walton. David Walton. But he doesn't know me."

"Do you live here?" she asked.

"Yes," David said quickly. "Just above town. Do you know the old Stinson place? I just moved here last month."

She studied David for a moment. "I'm Dallas," she said, extending her hand. David half rose from the stool to shake her hand then sat back down. She noticed and seemed pleased.

"You from Texas?" David asked smiling.

"No," she said, warming up some, "Idaho. But my daddy liked the Dallas Cowboys. America's Team," she said, making a number one sign with her index finger. "Beats being called Cowboy, I guess."

David laughed.

"I'll give him a call for you," she said. She moved to the telephone and started to dial.

"I want to talk to him about his book," David said, reminding her. "The Hawthorne book."

She stood with her back to David, listening. "No answer," she said. Still holding the phone, she turned and said it again.

"There's no answer." She hung up and walked back behind the bar.

"When do you think you will see him?" David asked. "Maybe you could just tell him I'd like to talk to him. Or you could tell him where I live."

"Actually," she said, "I haven't seen him in awhile. He may be away."

"Does he ever come here?" David asked hopefully.

"Pretty often," she said, "but not regular. It might be worth waiting around awhile though."

"Thanks. I think I will," David said. "It might be a good time to catch him."

"More enchiladas?" Dallas asked, looking at his empty plate.

"No, thanks. But I will have another beer. Make it a Coors."

He took the beer can, turned off of the stool and walked to one of the tables. He wanted to put his feet up. He sat in one chair and put his feet in another just as two young men with acoustic guitars came through the door.

"Hey Dallas!" one of them called as they sat down in chairs by the piano.

"Evening guys," and as she said it she tossed a can of beer to each of them.

"Where's Claude?" asked one of the young men.

"He just left," she said. "You just missed him."

Claude played the piano with the two boys almost every night. He had been born in Henson and had never left except when he was drafted. He didn't stay long. He had been discharged after a month because he didn't have "enough personality." He still lived with his mother and he drank a lot. He could play blues piano, and everyone said he was the best in Colorado.

"Rudy! Hey, here's Rudy," said the taller guitar player, and slapped Rudy a high-five as he walked in. Rudy was sixty-two years old. If you had guessed Rudy was from west Texas – and you would have - you would have been right. He sat at the table next to David's and turned to face them.

"You guys at it again?" Rudy said.

"You bet, Rudy. Music makes it all better," said the tall guitar player tuning up. "You know that."

Rudy had been coming to Henson on fishing trips every summer for twelve years. Last year he sold his house in Pampa, and he and his wife moved into a trailer on the Gunther road while he built his new "home," as he called it. "The view is worth it all," he said.

The two boys with the guitars were helping him build the house. They had dropped out of college, and until Rudy came along, were living in a tent. When the house had come along far enough, Rudy and his wife had moved in and the boys had moved into the trailer.

"Hell, I give it to 'em," Rudy had told everybody. "It was old anyway, and they're good boys. You know they've got that trailer nearly full of books and not easy ones neither. I mean," he had paused for a word, "educational books," he had said with emphasis. "Lotsa' science. They read all night. When they're not playin'."

"Hydee," he said, turning to face David. "My name's Rudy Taylor." He offered his hand. Rudy was thin and looked all of sixty-two. Lots of wrinkles. Deep ones at the corners of his eyes and deeper horizontal ones across his forehead. His dentures clicked as he talked and his upper plate, which was a little too large, made his lip protrude slightly as if he had chewing gum tucked up under it. He was wearing a tired Phillips 66 "gimmie" cap pushed back on his head showing a hat line of sharp demarcation between the almost dead white of his upper forehead and his permanently sunburned face. His sport shirt was buttoned at the neck.

"David Walton." Rudy reached over and shook his hand.

"Glad to meet 'cha. Mind if I join ya?" he said, moving to David's table.

"Throw me a beer, Dallas." She had been waiting.

"You know," he said to David as if he had known him a lifetime, "I've learned a lot about these boys working with them." He gestured with his beer can toward the piano where

the boys were tuning their guitars. "I guess a lotta' people felt like I used to about kids with long hair and beards. Most of 'em probably on dope. Worthless. Dirty." As he talked, he picked a single filter Camel from the pack in his shirt pocket, lit it with a metal lighter, and snapped it shut. "But these kids here, they are good kids," he nodded toward them.

"You've got to take them one at a time," David volunteered.

"You're right. You're right." Rudy leaned forward on his elbows holding his cigarette with his hands under his chin. "Now you take that music," Rudy began. The tall guitar player was quietly picking out "Wildwood Flower". "I had no idea they could do that. They been living here all summer and I had no idea they could do that." He turned and was watching them. "Look at that fingerin'. You know," he said turning back to David, "when I was younger, I wanted to do that so bad I could taste it, but I never could get the hang of it. No amount of practicing would do. I worked on that thing nearly two years, but I never could get it. Nearly ruined my marriage. I finally give it to my boy."

"Wildwood Flower" had stopped.

"John," Rudy said, "play that one more time." Rudy got up, finished his beer standing, and walked over to the piano, putting his hand on the tall guitar player's shoulder.

"I've got to go to Gunther early in the mornin' so I've got to go now, but I would like to hear 'The Flower' one more time." He moved around in front of John so he could see his fingers and sat backwards in a straight chair.

"Come over here," he said motioning to David," so you can watch his fingers."

John played, picking out the runs carefully, smoothly.

"Idn't that sumthin'? Look at that." Rudy sat smiling, watching John's fingers, patting his foot, nodding his head at his favorite parts.

"Boy, that's sumthin," he said when John had finished. John looked up at Rudy, smiling appreciatively, nodding.

"Well, I'm goin'," Rudy said moving toward the door. "I'll see

you boys at the house tomorrow. Night", he said to David. Opening the door he looked back at John. "I don't know how you do it," he said shaking his head.

"It's the hair," John said with a grin.

5

Jack Fuller never showed up at the Pine Cone Thursday or Friday. David was reluctant to ask Dallas where his house was and she didn't volunteer it. She didn't volunteer his phone number either. If Fuller had called David, he had missed it.

David went back to the Pine Cone Saturday, but Fuller was not there. The war movie man was playing the old upright piano, moving from one song to the next, pausing just long enough to take a drink from the Coors can on the piano. Coors, David noted.

"Has Mr. Fuller been in?" David asked Dallas as he sat on the stool.

"No," she said. "Would you like for me to call him for you again?"

"Please. Thanks," David said.

Dallas went to the phone, dialed and waited. "Mr. Fuller? This is Dallas. You okay?" She nodded to David that he had said yes. "Just checking," she continued. "There's a man here who wants to talk to you about your book."

"The Hawthorne book," David coached her.

"The Hawthorne book," she repeated into the phone. "I don't know. He says he's been looking for you to talk to you about it. He's been down here for three nights hoping to run into you." She turned toward David as she talked.

David smiled and nodded affirmatively.

"Yes," she said, "he's right here. Just a second." She held out the phone to David. "He said, 'Put him on.' "

"Hello, Dr. Fuller? My name is David Walton. I'm interested in the Hawthorne Expedition. I read your book and I was hoping to have a chance to talk to you about it sometime. Would that be possible?"

David listened.

"No, I live here now," David said. "Yes, in Henson. I just moved here." He waited hopefully. "Well, actually anytime. Anytime is good for me." David didn't want to inconvenience the man he had waited so long to meet. "I would be happy to come to your place or..."

The voice on the other end of the line said for David to come to his house at ten o'clock the next morning. "That would be perfect," David said. "Yes. Capitol City. I know where that is. Yes. Thank you. I'll look forward to meeting you then. Good-bye."

"Thanks," David said smiling as he handed the phone back to Dallas. "You have been very helpful."

"No problem," she said graciously. "How about some enchiladas?"

"Good idea," David said.

"Red or green?"

David thought for a second. "Tonight I feel like celebrating. Make it both!"

"Christmas enchiladas coming right up!"

From Henson, it was fifteen miles up Acme Creek canyon to Capitol City. It was an abandoned ghost town and it had always been one of David's favorite places. He looked forward to the drive. Capitol City is where David would have wanted his house if it had not been for the bad road and the snowslides.

David left his cabin at nine o'clock and drove the two miles to Henson. At the south end of town he crossed the Acme Creek bridge and turned left following the creek upstream.

The creek had cut a deep, narrow canyon in the brown, volcanic breccias, and for the first few miles above town, the road was at the base of the cliffs along the side of the stream, matching it turn for turn. The road bed was made from crushed rock cut from the cliff face, then spread with a grader, forcing the creek into a narrow pocket-water channel.

Halfway up the canyon the valley widened to 200 yards and the road and the stream separated, the road bearing to the right up the wooded hillside. From this higher ground the peaks at the head of the valley were clearly visible, stacked so close together there didn't seem to be any room between them for the turnings of the creek or the road. Their rocky tops were bare and gray. Spruce and pine woods, dabbed with yellow blotches of turning aspen at the lower altitudes, rose quickly up

the steep slopes to push at the timberline like dark green fingers.

On both sides of the valley, reddish-yellow mine dumps and glory holes, little burrows, dotted the steep slopes. Long, slender fan-shaped scars, rocky and bare except for a few stunted bushes and aspen, all bent downhill, marked the avalanche tracks clearly. Water from the high-shaded snowpack trickled down some of the rocky tracks, around the broken trees and the rusty remains of twisted culverts, and passed under the road.

Above the peaks the morning sky looked like blue enamel. There was not a single cloud. There wouldn't be any clouds until afternoon when the mountains tossed up the warmer air. On summer days, when the air was warm, the cumulus puffs bloomed and turned gray on the bottoms and dumped quick showers with a regularity that you could set your watch by. Then just as quickly, the sky cleared and the road was dusty again. But now in September with the cooler air, there was less risk of midday thunderstorms, which at stream level were a nuisance but in the high country could be deadly.

The directions were pretty much as Fuller had said. His house was the first house on the right just above Capitol City. It was the only house above Capitol City. It was the only building above Capitol City, unless you counted Rose's Cabin, an old stage stop which hadn't been occupied for seventy-five years.

Capitol City wasn't a city anymore, and it had never been the capitol John Barnes had wanted it to be. Barnes had founded it with gold money from the Ajax Mine and Golden Fleece Mine and vowed that it would become the state capitol. Good thing it wasn't. It was fifteen miles above Henson on a rough, winding canyon road that was closed most of the winter except for snowmobiles. The only other way out was over Badger Pass, the old stage road that was passable only in the summer and then only by four-wheel drive.

The old town site was in a small meadow. It was always a surprise to enter it so suddenly. Here the canyon was gone, spreading quickly back away from the road to make room for the grassy park, a mile long and maybe a quarter mile wide. There was scarcely room enough for a town. Willows and alders grew along the stream that, quiet now, turned and returned through the meadow. Close on all sides, mountains rose above the horizon halfway to the vertical.

The buildings of the old town were completely gone, all torn down for firewood, or moved off as private cabins except for the Barnes' house. Three-story red brick, it stood at the east end of the meadow, next to the stream, just where it flowed from the meadow and entered the narrow part of the canyon. The old house was the first thing you saw when you entered the valley. The walls were three bricks thick, and the story was that Barnes had them hauled in on burros from Leadville, at a dollar a brick. But now the roof and the wooden upper floors had fallen in, tourists had taken away the "dollar bricks" that had fallen from the walls, and willows had grown up through the rotted floorboards to the height of the second floor.

Fuller's log house was to the right of the road, up an open slope in an aspen grove. A porch ran across the front of the house from side-to-side and behind that were large glass windows facing the sunset.

"Hello." They shook hands at the door. "I'm David Walton."

"Jack Fuller, come in."

David had expected an older man. A professor. The man who greeted him at the door was about fifty, David guessed. He was trim and fit. His tanned face suggested someone who had spent his life outdoors. He looks like a cowboy, thought David, more at home in a feedlot than a freshman class.

"I got your card," Fuller said, as he sat and motioned for David to sit on the other sofa facing the windows.

"It's very nice of you to see me on such short notice," David said, a little uneasy. "I'm afraid I have a long list of questions that I have been saving to ask you if we ever met."

"Well, the Hawthorne story is a good one." Fuller brushed his hand back over his graying widow's peak, a gesture he would make often. "Do you teach?"

"No, I just got interested in the expedition. Sort of accidently, actually." David added, "I enjoyed your book."

"It had pretty limited distribution, I'm afraid. How did you hear about it?" His eyes were blue, and kind.

"I saw it listed in Talbot's book on Ed Kirk," David said, pleased with himself. "Talbot cited your book as a reference."

"Oh, yes. Good book." He paused. "Did you say on the phone that you live here?"

"Well, sort of," David admitted. "I'm giving it a try. I was a physician. I've retired, and I moved up here to see how I would like it. I've been coming to Henson since I was a kid." Fuller didn't seem as impressed as David had hoped he would be. "The Hawthorne Expedition has been a sort of hobby of mine. I thought after I retired I might keep fiddling with it some. Maybe even write something for a magazine. I have been the most interested in what Hawthorne's actual route was. There's not much written about that, at least not that I could find. It's such a riddle. I keep thinking that there are enough clues to solve it. You know, like a good mystery novel." He looked at Fuller to see if he agreed.

"For instance if Hawthorne was really headed for the 'headwaters of the Rio Grande', as he said, it has always seemed to me that Spring Creek Pass would have been the natural route to take. No one has considered that, at least that I know of. You didn't deal much with their route in your book."

"I was more interested then in Hawthorne's presidential aspirations," Fuller explained. "The expedition was just a part of that. If he had succeeded on that expedition, he would have been the darling of the Manifest Destiny crowd. Perfect timing."

"What do you think happened?" David asked. "It seems so strange that someone with Hawthorne's experience could get lost. He had been all over the West. And his guide, he was supposed to know every foot of the Rocky Mountain country."

"Have you read the Kirk diaries?" Fuller said, leaning back in the sofa.

"Yes," David said. He was pleased Fuller had asked. "Actually, I saw them at the Huntington Library. I saw the original manuscripts." Fuller's eyebrows rose slightly. "I asked a friend at the university to write a letter of introduction for me. He had been badgering me for years to buy season hockey tickets, so I told him I would if he wrote the letter for me. It was some letter! He said I was an *expert* on Western Indians. I got the red carpet treatment." David laughed. Fuller was not amused.

David continued quickly. "I had read Dellen's book, and Halten's and Bullock's, but it was seeing those diary manuscripts that really stimulated my interest in the route the expedition followed. If you could be sure of the route they intended to take and the route they actually took, it

would shed a lot of light on who was to blame for the disaster." David leaned forward for emphasis. "Do you think Hawthorne was trying to cross the mountains where he did because he was too proud to listen to Walker?" Then without waiting for an answer, "If so, why did he pick Walker to guide him in the first place? Or did Walker just get lost or forget the way? That's hard to believe."

"Or did Walker intentionally lead them astray?" Fuller smiled.

David was surprised. He had never considered that. "Why would he do that?"

"The gear they had with them on the expedition must have been worth thousands of dollars," Fuller explained. "Ten thousand dollars some say. Suppose they had to abandon it. Walker could return in the spring and salvage it. Pretty good haul for a trapper who was used to taking in $150 in a good year. He was quite a scoundrel."

"Seems pretty risky even for a scoundrel," David said skeptically.

Fuller smiled and stood up. "I've got something you will be interested in."

David watched Fuller walk to the other end of the large room that was living room, study, and kitchen. Tidy for a bachelor, David thought as he looked around. Fuller took something from a large crowded bookshelf, and when he returned, he had a book and a packet of photographs. He sat on the sofa beside David and opened the book on the table between them. He turned the pages deliberately until he found what he wanted, then pushed the open book to David so he could see it. On both pages were color plates of watercolors.

"Remember these?" Fuller said.

"Sure," said David, leaning closely over the book. "This is..." he took a quick look at the cover of the book to confirm his suspicion, "Talbot's book. These are some of the watercolors Ed Kirk did on the expedition."

"Right. Look at this." Fuller sorted through the photographs, selected one, and after looking at it, lay the photograph on the open book alongside one of the watercolor prints. Both the watercolor and the photograph depicted a winter scene on a frozen stream with an unusual rock outcropping along the right side of the stream. A large mountain was in the background. The scenes were identical.

"Where did you get this photograph?" David asked, holding the photo, amazed.

"I took it myself. Look at this." Fuller lay another photograph beside the other open page. Another match.

"Where's this?" David said, amazed.

"About seventy-five miles from here."

"But, how...?"

"When I was at the college, I spent a lot of time prowling around the mountains. Fishing. Hiking. When I saw these watercolors in Talbot's book, I knew exactly where they were done. I had fished that stream many times. This rock bank is very unusual. Look at the shape." He pointed as he talked. "And the mountain in the background. I went in there in the winter and took these pictures from the same vantage point."

"Amazing," David said, holding a photograph in each hand and looking back and forth from the photographs to the book. "What stream is this?"

"Conejos Creek."

David looked at Fuller, astonished. "The Conejos Creek near Varden Peak?"

"The same," Fuller smiled. David noticed that Fuller's teeth were stained. He had a habit of covering them with his hand when he smiled.

David looked back at the photographs, then at Fuller. "Do you know anything about the stumps on Varden Peak that are supposed to be campsites?" David asked hopefully.

"I've never seen them myself," Fuller said, "but they are Hawthorne's campsites, I'm sure of it. It fits the description in the diaries."

"Then, you think, Hawthorne went up Conejos Creek to Varden Peak where they were stranded in the snow?" David said.

"It's the only way they could have come to the place where these watercolors were made." He tapped the book with his finger. "Kirk sure didn't do any sketches on the way down. They were all dying by then."

"The Conejos Creek route makes so much more sense," David said, sitting back, agreeing. "Bullock said in his book that Hawthorne was headed for a pass at the headwaters of the Rio Grande but missed it. That he turned too soon up Willow Creek, but I never could buy that. Turning up at Willow Creek would have meant that they had not yet passed Weminuche Gap, twelve miles farther up the river. Even in the

winter they couldn't have missed Weminuche Gap. There's no place else in that valley like it."

"Bullock was wrong," Fuller said bluntly. "He didn't have the watercolors. Besides, he didn't know the country. He only spent four days there."

"And everyone has quoted him since," David suggested.

"You've got it."

"I can't believe these photographs!" David said looking at them again. "They're incredible."

"Re-read the diaries. Everything fits Conejos Creek canyon. The 'series of canyons', the 'friable volcanic formations, the pine ridges'. Go take a look. The cliffs at the mouth of the creek forced them over to the south bank - the 'hills sparsely covered with small piñon pines'. It's possible that they were trying to cut north to intersect Coalbank Pass, although that doesn't make too much sense. Walker had already tried to convince Hawthorne not to take Coalbank Pass because of the deep snow there. Anyway," he continued, "by keeping to the south side of the stream they would have missed the north fork of Conejos stream that would have taken them over the ridge to the Coalbank. But several streams come together there. And the weather was terrible. Whatever," he continued, "following Conejos Creek would have led them up the flank of Varden Peak..."

"Where the campsites are!" David interrupted.

"Exactly."

"When did you put all this together?"

"Right after Talbot's book was published. When I saw those watercolors, it all clicked."

"Have you published these yet?" David said, holding up the photographs.

"Not yet."

David felt relieved. "But how did those watercolors ever survive?" he asked. "No one made it down from the mountains except Hawthorne and Walker. It doesn't seem likely that either one of them carried watercolors out. Hawthorne even left all of his baggage."

"Who knows," Fuller agreed. "Talbot said he bought them from a couple in Pennsylvania who had found them in a garage."

"For that matter," David asked, "how did Kirk's diaries survive?"

"No one seems to know," Fuller said with a shrug. "They just turned up nearly seventy-five years later in a collection of rare books which sold in New York in 1921. The owner of the gallery said he had bought the lot from a man named Anderson in Chicago, but no one has been able to trace them before that, at least not that I am aware of. When it was recognized what they were, the diaries were donated to the Huntington Library, where you saw them. Some said that the suggestion that these papers were the ones that had been abandoned in the mountains was pretty fanciful, but there they are."

"No question about that," David said. He was looking out the window at the mountains. "But, if they went up Conejos Creek, what about the 'headwaters of the Rio Grande'?" He turned to Fuller for a response. "In that letter to his wife, that's where Hawthorne said he was headed, didn't he? He said he intended to cross the mountains at the headwaters of the Rio Grande. Conejos Creek is not the headwaters of the Rio Grande."

"The idea we have now of the headwaters may be much too narrow," Fuller explained. "In 1848 the headwaters of the Rio Grande may have included not only the main river but also tributaries to the north such as Conejos Creek and even Coalbank Creek. No explorers known to Hawthorne had been to the headwaters of the Rio Grande, you know."

"Yes," David said carefully, "but I did see a map at the National Archives, the map Heath did when he came through the Antonio Valley in 1851, two years after Hawthorne. Probably you know the map. It shows the Rio Grande about where modern day maps do, clearly south of Conejos Creek." David hoped he wasn't being offensive.

"That's true," Fuller agreed, "but the map Gunther made in 1853, just a year later, shows the headwaters of the Rio Grande arising in the Coalbank Pass, north of Conejos Creek, and even including it. I'm afraid the old mapmakers weren't as good as we would like them to be. If you look at enough of the maps of that period, you see the same mistakes copied from one map to the next."

"Like the historians' theories?" David teased cautiously.

Fuller smiled. "If they don't do the original field research themselves." He accentuated "field" heavily.

"But the Kirks' diaries," David argued, "they clearly indicate that they thought they were on the Rio Grande. One diary even referred

to reaching 'the thickly-timbered river.' The Rio Grande is lined with cottonwoods. As I remember it Conejos Creek is a small stream that disappears into the soil of the valley just after leaving the mountains. It would be hard even in winter to confuse these two today."

"Today," Fuller emphasized, "is the operative word. In the 1870s, when the Antonio Valley was being settled the banks of Conejos Creek, where it entered the valley, had enough trees to be known as 'the bottoms.' Besides," he continued, "the distances are all wrong. That's the thing that bothered me for the longest time. When Hawthorne's men reported seeing trees along a river seven miles away, they were right about the distance. I have checked that several times, and seven miles is about the distance stands of trees are visible in the valley. But the trees they saw couldn't have been the trees along the Rio Grande. I made the same mistake all the others had made. Just like the historians who said Hawthorne went to the Rio Grande, I had ignored Kirk's diary entries describing the two day detour to cross the north end of the sand dunes on the east side of the valley."

"But what about that entry in Heath's diary?" David was prying politely, trying not to be offensive. "I remember the description because it was so colorful. Heath was camped on the Rio Grande on July the 4th, near what sounds like the present site of Monte Vista. He said that the sun was setting behind the pass in the San Juans, at the head of the Rio Grande, 'in which Hawthorne met with so terrible a disaster'. Wasn't he referring to a pass at the headwaters of the Rio Grande, like Spring Creek Pass, rather than Conejos Creek?"

"Well, as a matter of fact, in early July from that vantage point, the sun sets not to the west but to the northwest, directly behind Varden Peak, at the head of Conejos Creek." Fuller smiled.

David was pleased. All this was more than he had hoped for. Fuller obviously knew a lot about the expedition. Living in the area while he taught at the college had allowed him to check out leads firsthand, and he was proud of his field work.

Fuller brought out maps and together they studied them, sometimes with a magnifying glass for details they might have missed. Fuller explained the route he thought the expedition had taken and how the survivors had come down out of the mountains.

The two men got along well. They talked for most of the afternoon,

enjoying the mutual flattery of their shared interest. David had worried that an expert like Fuller might not take him seriously. That he might be resentful of an amateur. Or that he would be aloof, or secretive about his work. But Fuller was impressed with the time David had spent, his thoroughness and his ideas, and he seemed to enjoy the discussion rather than to be threatened by the questions.

David left before dark, making excuses about why he could not stay longer. He wanted to stay, and Fuller encouraged him, but he was afraid that he would overstay his welcome. Also he was excited about what he had learned. He felt that he had to leave before he was overloaded, to be quiet and to think over all he had learned. The drive back to Henson was perfect for that.

TUESDAY, DECEMBER 31

Today was occupied beating a trail back over the ridge. The trail formed a trench through the snow 9 ft. deep in places, wide at the top, narrowing to 1 ft. at the bottom. All day the caravan of black figures moved single file through this winding gap, relaying the baggage. We passed and repassed the bodies of the frozen mules, humps in the snow. Our camp is in a canyon 50 ft. wide and filled with snow. Only the tops of the tallest trees are visible. The men have scooped out large holes in the snow and sit with their feet towards the fire, their blankets over their heads. The thermometer stands at 10 degrees below zero and the wind, strong all day, funnels down through the canyon from the summit with hurricane strength.

Breaking the trail through the deep snow was laborious, especially at this altitude where breathing is so difficult, and the men are exhausted. They are quite depressed over Walton's death, even though we were not surprised by it. Never in all the winters I have spent in the mountains have I seen storms as continuous and as severe as these. None of the rigors of mountain travel tries men more than snow. The depth and the relentlessness of it sap the strength and the morale equally. Perhaps the men's spirits will rise now that we are turned back. Even my dark and anxious thoughts of yesterday are lifting. I am now thankful for that forboding for it inspired me to turn back from that camp where we would have all surely perished and I am convinced that we shall in the end prevail.

Having secures the lives of the men, we will go quickly back down to the river and then to the settlements and with fresh animals and supplies, we shall cross through the Sierra by a different route. It will be strenuous, but I am not discouraged. Our mission has to this point only been delayed and I shall carry it on uninterrupted. The present situation offers no choices but to sink under this tide of misfortune or, by strenuous endeavor, rise above it.

6

The sky was just getting pink when David saw Dub drive up. He had been watching for him and had seen his truck coming up the hill before he could hear it. They wanted to get an early start because of the long ride. David had already eaten breakfast, but he knew Dub would have coffee in the truck and Jolene's cinnamon rolls.

Dub had already hitched the horse trailer behind the pickup. The morning air was cold, and the warm vapors of the horses' breath puffed rhythmically out between the trailer's metal slats.

"Morning, Dub," David said, sliding into the truck. The heater felt good. He could smell the rolls.

"Mornin', Doc. Jolene sent you these." Dub pushed a paper sack toward him on the seat. "Made 'em this mornin'." The rolls were better than he had remembered. The thick white sugar icing had melted and run down into the spiraled rolls. They were even better the next day David recalled.

Steering with one hand and holding his coffee cup with the other, Dub turned left onto the highway. The mountains at the south end of the valley were black silhouettes against the light sky. They drove toward the mountains, three miles past Dub's place to the upper end of the valley where the road turned and began to ascend the steep pass, climbing and winding, switching back on itself as it rose through aspen and pine forests.

The mountain pass road was paved, but David remembered the first time he had come over it in the back seat of his family's 1941 Plymouth two-door sedan. It was a gravel road then, and only one lane wide, much of it shelf road. Where it was possible passing areas

had been cut from the steep banks. If two cars met between these passing areas, the uphill car had to back up until the road was wide enough for the cars to pass. The car straining uphill had the right-of-way. If it stopped, it might stall.

That first trip had been at night in a driving rain. The windshield wipers of the old Plymouth didn't work when the car was pulling the steep grades, and David's father had kept his head out the window in the rain for thirty miles trying to keep the edge of the road in sight. His mother prayed and urged David and his brother, who were on the floor of the backseat, their heads covered with their colorbooks, to do the same.

"Boy, I'll never forget the first time I came over this pass," David said.

Dub laughed. "That was the night I tried to rent your dad the chicken house."

"We were pretty scared," David recalled.

"Your father told me later that he hadn't thought it would take that long to get over the pass. He said he looked at the map at Antelope Park and saw that it was only fifty-six miles and thought he could make it before dark. He hadn't had much experience driving in the mountains."

"It must have impressed him," David agreed. "For years after that we avoided the pass by going all the way around and coming in from Gunther."

Dub laughed again. "That was a bad way to start. I'm surprised you ever came back." He put his empty coffee cup in a cupholder on the dashboard and lit his first cigar. "By golly, Doc, this a pretty place. Aren't you glad you kept coming back?"

"I wouldn't trade it for anything."

Dub was wearing his hat, a stained old silver-belly Stetson pushed back on his head as if he had forgotten it was there. It was the only hat David had ever seen him wear.

"In the 1870s, the army came through here," Dub said, steering. "Four or five years before Henson was a town. A Lieutenent Ruffner. He was on a reconnaissance through the Ute country for the War Department. Wasn't long before they had run all the Indians off to Utah. Ruffner came right over this pass." Dub watched the road as he talked, steering the truck around the tight turns. "It was an old

Indian trail then, from Los Alamos to the Ute's wintering grounds over at Pagosa. When it came time to build the road the highway department just followed the trail. Didn't even have to change the grades."

"The topographical maps show this as a natural pass," David said.

"Those Indians knew what they were doing," Dub stressed. His cigar, parked in the corner of his mouth, had already gone out.

At the summit of the pass, Dub pointed out a road that turned off to the left. "That's probably the way Packwood walked out," he said. "It leads down to the Ute camp at Los Alamos. Must be forty miles."

David tried to visualize himself walking forty miles in the winter at that altitude. He had always been amazed at some of the things those exceptional men had attempted. It was hard for David to imagine walking the distances they walked, living outside in danger without the conveniences he would consider minimal, intentionally traveling, often without maps or charts, to places with which they were not familiar. But to set out on foot to cross the mountains in the winter was almost beyond comprehension. Beyond the summit of the pass the road wound down through the forested slopes, and it was easy to make out the distinct growth zones dictated by the altitude. Spruce and fir, capable of withstanding late springs and early frosts, grew at the highest altitude where rainfall was the greatest and water was plentiful. Two thousand feet lower down on the sunny drier slopes, the fir and spruce give way to the ponderosa pine. In the mountains it was easy to tell the altitude from the type of trees.

"Ruffner said this side of the pass was the the easiest grade over the Divide in the southern Rockies," Dub said. "Just look at it." A perfect place for Hawthorne to cross, David thought.

In order, they had left the fir and spruce, and then the pine. They passed through a rolling, hummocky highland with grassy parks and clumps of aspen growing in the looser soil of the hillsides and then descended in a broad, U-shaped valley, gray-green with sage. Ahead on the left, standing like a giant stockade, the volcanic columnar cliffs of Bristol Head marked the uppermost end, the headwaters, of the Rio Grande Valley.

At Bristol Head the road joined the river flowing east toward the Antonio Valley forty miles away. Just past the basalt cliffs of Weminuche Gap they turned north into the mountains. It was nine

o'clock when Dub bumped the truck to a stop at the end of the dirt road.

They had followed the road from where it turned off the highway up a wooded canyon as far as they could go in the truck. Dub led the horses from the trailer and easily saddled them both. He pulled up into the saddle, and leading the dappled gray horse, rode over to where David sat, handing him the reins.

"Here Doc," he said around the cigar, "you take old Bonnie. I can tell she likes you. Even if she doesn't you'll be pretty good friends by the end of the day."

David rode in behind Dub, following him up the game trail. The canyon narrowed quickly, and as they rode through the trees Bonnie's saddle squeaked rhythmically with each step. It was a perfect day, cool and bright. No snow David thought. The last of the wild lettuce bloomed bright yellow in the grass along the stream bank. The aspen had turned, and in the light breeze, their leaves quaked like gold medallions. Ahead beyond the turning valley sides, slanting left and right, was the bare, gray top of Varden Peak, in full sun against the cloudless sky.

"By golly Doc, this is the only way to travel," Dub said over his shoulder.

He's right, David thought. The pace of a horse's walk is perfect, just fast enough to get where you need to go and slow enough so you can see the country you are riding through.

Within an hour they were at 11,000 feet nearly out of the trees. Of all places in the mountains this was David's favorite. There, just below timberline, the sub alpine spruce were widely spaced. Old brown logs lay broken on the sunny ground. The underbrush was gone giving way to clumps of tawny, tufted grass and thrifty bushes with the small leaves and low profiles that protected them from the drying winds.

In the summer wildflowers covered the high country in the wet places like a multicolored afghan — primrose, gilia, Indian paintbrush, purple fringe, queen's crown, flax, wild geranium, lupine, buttercups. Now with the shortening days, the flowers were all gone except for here and there, a columbine, their exothermic pigment deepest blue where they grew in the shade.

David and Dub rode slowly up the rocky ridge that connected the

double crest of the mountain. At the top of the ridge Dub stopped, turned in his saddle, and said something to David that was lost in the thin air.

David rode up beside him. "There they are," Dub said, pointing.

"I'll be damned," David breathed. "It's just like they said." Down over the barren ridge on the eastern facing slope were several tall, silver stumps and a small clump of fir trees. Hawthorne's Christmas Camp.

The old stumps stood like totems, wooden testimonials. For David they were the first physical confirmation of what, until then, had been only a terrible tale. David's mind leaped the 150-year gap like a spark. There on the side of that desperate ridge among the trees and stumps, the figures of the men in the books took shape, dark forms against the snow. Wrapped in blankets, huddled motionless against the wind around their smokey fire pits, they waited, figures in an eerie, white tabloid.

Somewhere on that hillside, in the cold of that unbearable Christmas, Matthew Walton had died. Overcome by their own efforts to survive and unable to summon the strength to bury him, the other men had left his body in the snow, lying where he had fallen.

"Want to go down and take a look?" Dub said.

David nodded.

Picking their way over the rocky ground, David and Dub rode down to the campsite, dismounted and and tied the horses. Most of the old stumps had fallen over and lay scattered down the hillside like the bones of a large animal. Six of the stumps were still standing. David stood by one of them and touched its gray smoothness. He could not reach the top. Beyond it were five others nearly the same height. Almost equally spaced in two parallel lines of three, the six stumps formed a rough rectangle, the same gruesome geometry of the six white posts that marked the site of the Packwood graves.

The two men spent an hour wandering around the old campsite. Dub showed David where he had seen the mule bones, but they couldn't find any, either among the trees and stumps, or down the slope below the campsite where they might have been carried by slides or the spring run-off.

Dub related to David how Simpson had told him about a rancher moving cattle over the ridge in the 1930s, who had found an old wooden shovel and a bunch of brass rings. He claimed to have seen a McClellan packsaddle in a tree and had planned to go back and get it but never did. He also told Simpson that he had seen an inscription, "1848," carved on a rock nearby, but no one else had ever been able to find it.

Tired but not wanting to leave, the two men sat in the cool sunshine on one of the fallen stumps and talked while they ate lunch.

"I guess this is where they spent their most dismal day," David said. "Christmas Day 1848. One of the Kirks said in his diary that at noon it was was twenty degrees below zero, and the wind was blowing the snow into a pouderrie that obliterated the sky. Most of the men had frozen fingers and feet. At times, blood oozed from their lips and noses and froze on their faces. Their fires melted deep holes in the snow. They tried to sleep in these holes, to get out of the wind, but the thick smoke burned their eyes. All around them was the litter of packs and baggage. Dead and dying mules lay where they had fallen in the night. Others, their manes and tails chewed off, brayed and raced wildly about in the deep snow, crazed with the cold. They were finished, and they knew it."

"Hard to imagine, isn't it, Doc?" Dub said, folding his arms across his chest, shaking his head.

"Apparently for days at a time it was nearly impossible to travel. They spent hours pounding the deep snow with mauls they had made from tree trunks, just to make a trail barely a hundred yards long which the storms covered over completely by the next day. They prayed for the weather to break, but it never did. After five horrible days Hawthorne finally gave up, here. Christmas Camp, they called it."

"Sounds more like Camp Dismal," Dub suggested. "How'd they ever get down from here?"

"Hawthorne decided to try to return to the river as quickly as possible. Somehow the men rallied," David continued, "but by that time several of the men had already died. They just left them in the snow. Didn't have the strength to bury them. When they left here, they probably went back over that ridge," David turned and pointed back the way they had come down. "According to the diaries, they made only about

two hundred yards the first day. Just barely over the ridge. Things weren't much better there, but it was as far as they could go. The storms continued, one after another, and they were pinned down for days at a time. When the weather finally cleared, they started down toward the river."

"Did you say diaries?" Dub said.

"Some of the men on the expedition kept diaries," David said. "I've got copies of the diaries the two Kirk brothers kept."

Dub squinted. "But if they died up here..."

"How did the diaries turn up?" David finished.

"Right," Dub confirmed.

"Would you believe nobody know?"

Dub looked skeptical.

"It does seem strange, doesn't it?" Said David.

"It sure does," Dub agreed.

"That's just another one of the mysteries of that expedition. Somehow the diaries ended up in a library in California."

Dub was thinking that over when David said," Come on, I'll show you how I think they went down from here."

They rode back up over the ridge and sat among the rocks. Varden Peak, a group of bare summits connected by ridges, sloped steeply away from them to the east. Immediately below where they sat, a broad, boulder-strewn field narrowed abruptly, just at the pointed timberline, into a series of wooded canyons, turning and descending into the Antonio Valley. On the other side of the valley fifty miles away, and blued by the distance, the serrated silhouette of the Sangre de Cristo Mountains stood propped against the horizon.

"Apparently as they came west, they crossed the Sangre de Cristos there," David explained, "just behind the sand dunes. Then they came over the dunes and headed northwest across the valley apparently headed for Coalbank Pass." He was pointing alternately to the landmarks in the valley and to the map he had unfolded on his knees.

"Then, for some reason, they turned and headed southwest."

"Why was that?" Dub asked.

"That's another one of the big controversies," David said. "Some

have thought they were originally trying to go over Coalbank Pass but changed their minds because there was too much snow. Others have thought that they were headed for the Rio Grande in the first place, planning to follow it to the headwaters and cross the Divide there, and that they just circled up to the north after trying to avoid this marshy area west of the dunes. If we knew the answer to that question we might know whose idea it was to come up here."

"What about the diaries?" Dub asked.

"Unfortunately they're not clear on that point. There's some evidence that Hawthorne insisted on coming this way, and there's some evidence that the guide just got lost."

"What about Hawthorne's diary?"

David looked at Dub and smiled. "Guess what?"

"What?" said Dub.

"It's never been found."

"Maybe he didn't keep one," Dub suggested.

"He kept one, all right," David assured him. "He kept a diary on every expedition he ever went on. This one just disappeared."

"I see," Dub said with mock surprise, smiling. "Well, after they turned south, what happened then?"

"In the open valley they nearly froze. They were exposed to the wind, and there wasn't any firewood. One day the temperature was so low that the mercury never rose out of the bulb of the thermometer. Even in the valley the snow was deep. Before they left Pueblo one of the guides Hawthorne had tried to hire said he had never seen so much snow that early in the year and refused to go."

"That would have been clue enough for me," Dub said matter-of-factly.

"Well, they went anyway. Hawthorne said he wanted to cross the mountains in the winter to prove that the railroad could operate year 'round. They almost froze in that blizzard in the valley. As if things weren't bad enough, one night all their mules got loose and they had to run them all down."

"I'd have packed it up!" Dub snorted, shifting his feet further back under him and crossing his arms on his knees.

"From the diaries it sounds like they struck Conejos Creek about there," David pointed, "and followed it up that flank of the

mountain to where we are sitting." He didn't tell Dub about Fuller and the photographs.

"Just where the hell did they think they were going?" Dub asked, amazed.

"That part's not clear. Some think they were trying to cut back over to Coalbank Pass."

"Cut across up the North Fork of the creek?"

"Right. You can just see it there," he pointed out a branching of Conejos Creek.

"You mean they changed their minds again!"

"Either that or got crossed up somewhere down in the canyon and missed the turn. It was still storming. Maybe they couldn't see all that well," David offered.

"Can you imagine!" Dub said, exasperated. "Why didn't they just follow the Rio Grande to Spring Creek Pass, back along the way we came here this morning? It would have been a damn sight easier."

"Looks like it to me, too," said David, "and some think that's where they may have been headed, and that they just got confused. When they hit Conejos Creek maybe they thought it was the Rio Grande and followed it 'til it was too late."

"Only two of 'em got down from here, didn't they?" Dub said. "Hawthorne and the guide?"

"Right," said David. "When they left Christmas Camp and started back down to the river they probably tried to move the baggage down one of these canyons." David indicated the canyon just to the right of the one they had ridden up.

"Baggage!" Dub said, disbelieving.

"Hawthorne wanted the baggage out."

"And that dimwit was almost president!"

David laughed. Fuller would like Dub, he thought. "They tried to slide the baggage down, but the canyon was too steep, so they had to retrace their steps back, maybe over this way." David was looking at a map now. "Probably about the head of that ridge. The head of Pine Cone Creek. That took two days."

"Simpson said that there was another campsite at the head of Pine Cone Creek," Dub said. "You can't see it from here, but it's about... ah, there," he said, leaning over David's shoulder and pointing out

Pine Cone Creek on the map.

"I'm not sure exactly how they went, but by this time they were in real trouble. Lugging the baggage was exhausting them. The terrain was very difficult, and the storms had started again. The wind blew so hard at times the men had to lie down to keep from being blown over cliffs. What rations they had left gave out, and they began to eat anything they could find — rawhide ropes and shoe strings. Their parfleches. Once they found a dead wolf, one side of it and the intestines eaten away, but they ate it anyway. Roasted it and ate it, hair and all. Even the bones. By this time they had separated into small quarreling groups scattered down the valley. It was nearly everyone for himself. Several others had died. The diaries stopped. One on January 9th. The other on the 11th."

"Bro-ther!" Dub exclaimed. "All dead but Hawthorne and the guide. How'd they get out?"

"Hawthorne said they made it down the canyon to the river and then followed it down to near Blanco where some Mexicans found them. They were trying to get to Santa Fe or Taos."

"Blanco must be 150 miles from here," Dub said. "They're frozen and starving, and they walked 150 miles!"

"They're just lucky somebody found them," David said.

The two men were talking when the storm came up. It came up from behind them so quickly that David and Dub were completely surprised. Neither of them had noticed the change in the color of the sky. They hadn't noticed the change in the temperature or the little breeze that came up and then stopped.

The lightning and the thunder crack came at the same instant. Then another, and another in quick succession. It was deafening. Dub said later that it was like having your head in a washtub that someone was beating on with a pump handle.

The first thunder had not only startled the men but the horses as well. David had tied Bonnie's reins to a stick he had brought up the mountain with them. Dub said it was all Bonnie needed to make her think she was tied. With the first thunder Bonnie flinched and backed up and went down on her hindquarters. When she did the stick flew around her on the end of the rein and struck her on the flank. Wild-eyed, she jumped and spun around, the stick swinging suddenly from out of her visual field around her head. Terrified, she scrambled to escape the swinging stick. The lightning and thunder were almost continuous. In the flashing light and the booming, the horse completely lost control. She tore off wildly down the boulder field, pitching and tossing her head and swinging the stick, trying to dodge it as she ran.

"Get down," Dub yelled into the wind, and David did. The noise was unbearable. Hail the size of moth balls whitened the ground and pelted the men who covered their heads and curled under the rocks to try to avoid the stinging pellets. Then as quickly as it had come, the hail changed to cold torrents of wind-driven rain that soaked through their coats. The rocks around the men were ringed with a faint bluish light and hummed like high-pitched transformers. The sky was greenish-black.

And then it was gone. The lightning stopped first. Then the rain slowed and stopped. It was very quiet, except for the thunder which grumbled occasionally off to the east. The smell of ozone was strong. David peeped up over a rock to see Dub peeping up over a rock.

"How'd you like that, Doc," he smiled.

"THAT was a thunderstorm!" Said David.

"You still in one piece?" Dub said, as he got stiffly to his feet, flipped the water off his hat against his pants leg and made his way over to where David sat. "You all right?"

David was shaken. "I think so."

"Told you they was humdingers," Dub said, trying to be helpful. "Humdingers," he said again. He stood by the rock where David sat and looked out at the storm. The dark cloud had moved down off the mountain and was dragging a gray veil of rain across the valley. The sun lit the billowed, white anvil top.

"Let's get out of here. I'm freezing. I could use a drink, and them damn horses ran off with the whisky." He helped David to his feet, and together they made their way slowly down through the rocks.

By the time they reached the truck two hours later, the men had warmed up. Both the horses were grazing by the stream as if nothing had ever happened, apparently no worse off for the experience except that both of Bonnie's reins were broken off short.

"It's a wonder you didn't break your fool neck," Dub said to Bonnie

as he loaded her into the trailer.

Dub joined David in the truck, lit a cigar, then started the motor and drove off. They didn't talk as they followed the bumpy, rutted, Forest Service road down through the trees. When they turned onto the highway and back toward Henson, the sun was nearly down and the sky was clear, except in the west where the clouds had been swept into a line and set afire.

7

David drove slowly through the little town to the end of Gunther Avenue, turned and came back up Silver Street. It was early Sunday morning and almost no one was out. The sheriff's blue Bronco was parked in front of the Pine Cone. A few dogs, like old men dressed in different clothes, were making their rounds. It was good to be back in Henson, he thought.

The town fit neatly in the little ellipse of the mountain valley. Two main streets lined with old cottonwoods ran nearly due north and south along the west branch of the Gunther River. Acme Creek entered the valley from the west, flowed through the town dividing it into two nearly equal halves, then joined the river and was lost.

David had always supposed the cottonwoods grew there naturally. Later when he learned that they had been planted he was surprised. Surprised and a little embarrassed, that he had been naive enough to think of the early settlers as too preoccupied with survival to be concerned with aesthetics.

The shaded houses were unchanged and just as he remembered them, western mountain mix — log cabins, painted Victorian frame with gingerbread porches, long, thin two-story bricks with Romanesque arched windows. There was a tin-roofed motel behind the armory on Bluff Street, the green and white frame two – story courthouse, the trailer park by the river bridge, the Presbyterian church and a laundromat.

Henson had been settled in the summer of 1875. It was that spring that the luckless Packwood had wandered out of the little valley to the Indian agency at Los Alamos. In July prospectors had found the five bodies, the shallow graves partially dug by animals, and by August, gold.

The gold strike at Henson had been a big one. High grade ore was discovered in the hills and canyons all around the town. Within two weeks it was a tent city of two thousand people. Cabins and rough shacks were hastily thrown up, and what streets existed were narrow, muddy trails winding among the crude buildings. The town grew so fast that it was said that the oldest resident would scarcely recognize the town after a week's absence. Before the boom ended there were five thousand people living in the little valley, and the newspaper boasted of among other things: ten assayers, two banks, two pool halls, two breweries, two cigar factories, five stables, fourteen general stores, four Chinese laundries, seven saloons – two open all night – and a Red Light District on Bluff Street.

But there was no mining left. When the mines played out most of the people who hadn't died of smallpox moved on, leaving a population, as Dub put it, of "a hundred and forty-four when they were all home." There were a few ranch families, a handful of retirees from the plains, and a few locals catering to the tourist trade.

The buildings still standing were the ones which hadn't burned. The Wheeler Block, a row of boardwalk-connected false fronts, was what remained of Henson's business district, anchored at the north end by the two-story, brownstone Howe Bank, now the Elkhorn Bar on the first floor and the editorial offices of the Silver World upstairs. Next door the drugstore, home of "Malts like you used to get," boasted the oldest marble soda fountain on the Western Slope, "Brought in all the way from Oklahoma." The ice cream was still trucked in once a week from Salinas Creamery 125 miles away. Next to the drugstore, were the Alpine Gift Shop, the Henson Grocery & Sportsman, a failing art gallery, and beyond that, a building whose first tenant was Mrs. Hannenkalm's Millinery Shop, and its most recent, the "off-again-on-again" Henson Health Clinic.

Across the street from Wheeler Block was the one-square-block park that had been the site of the Pioneer Hotel. There's no one left who remembers the fire that destroyed it, but the newspaper accounts are impressive. Dub said his father told him that the building went up so fast that the dog didn't even get out. The only remnant of the hotel was the painted safe door that lay rusting in the grass, too heavy to steal.

The Pine Cone was on the north side of the park across the street and

next to a two-story brick building that, for awhile, was Mack's Grocery on the first floor and home of the Saturday night movie on the second. In the summers the Little Nell Theatre used it for melodramas. The Do Drop Inn cabins, matched little log houses, the cut ends of the logs painted white, backed up to the east side of the park. The only building left on the south end of the park was the old stone livery stable that Mrs. Epperson and the D.A.R. tried to convert into the Henson County Museum but couldn't.

David drove back by the park and crossed back over the Acme Creek bridge, where on a clear spring night in 1882, Andrew Browning and Clair Betts had been hanged by "unknown parties" for shooting Sheriff Campbell. The bodies had been left dangling from ropes for a full day, and school was dismissed so that the children "might view a demonstration that crime did not pay."

He followed the main road south back out of town, and after two miles he could see, on a rise across the river, the red roof of his cabin. It was a one-story cabin, very old, made from spruce logs that in the dry air had weathered the color of coffee. The covered porch on the front had sunset views up and down the valley. Sunsets were important in the West. David had missed sunsets in New Hampshire where everything seemed to be oriented toward the sunrise. The cabin had three bedrooms and a bath, the latter added with the plumbing, and a stone fireplace in the living room which was separated from the kitchen only by the kitchen table.

David parked beside the back door of the cabin, went inside and sat down at the kitchen table. The Forest Service map was still spread out on the table, a coffee cup on each corner. He sat at the table and studied the map thinking about what Fuller had told him. He was excited about what he had learned. The photographs were very impressive and really made the case for the Conejos Creek route.

David had been interested in the Hawthorne Expedition for a long time. Researching it had exercised the deductive skills he had honed as a physician. Even with his busy practice, he had made time for his quest and it had been a satisfying research project for him. After Susan's death, working on the Project, as he called it, had helped him through a bad time. Like a good book, he had savored it, watched it unfold slowly, saving the ending until he had the time to finish it, uninterrupted. Now he was disappointed that the chase seemed to be over so soon.

Researching the Hawthorne Expedition would have been a nice retirement project thought David. He would finally have had the time to do the field work. He had published one non-medical article, an edited collection of Civil War letters, but he was looking forward to using his retirement to write something about the expedition. Perhaps an article for a history magazine. Perhaps even a book. Now, almost certainly Fuller would.

Actually David realized even if Conejos Creek was the route the expedition took into the mountains, there was still the question of who was to blame for the disaster. The real issues remained. Why did they choose that route, and who chose it? It was very risky to try to cross the San Juans at that point in the winter, and the route they chose was not suitable for the railroad in any season.

David reviewed the possibilities as he had many times before. Hawthorne may have actually intended to ascend "the headwaters of the Rio Grande" and cross the mountains at the 38th parallel as he said. If he had misplaced his faith in Walker, who became lost, or led them astray intentionally as Fuller had suggested, it would implicate Walker. On the other hand Hawthorne, as leader of the expedition, may have overruled Walker and urged the fatal route on him. With the weather as bad as it was, even a skilled guide like Walker could not have abandoned the expedition to head back alone. He would have been forced to go along and try to make the best of it.

Alternatively Hawthorne certainly did have a flair for the dramatic, and "the headwaters of the Rio Grande" may have been only a romantic notion. Perhaps he planned to head for the general region of the headwaters of the Rio Grande, an area where neither he nor any of his party except perhaps Walker, had ever been, and merely find his way when he got there.

It really all boiled down to intent. Unfortunately there was no complete record of the disastrous mountain adventure. The Kirk diaries dealt primarily with their own perceptions, descriptions of the weather and the country, and daily mileages. If they were aware of discussions of the plans or the routes, they did not seem concerned, nor did they make note of it. Walker is said to have kept a diary, but it had never been found.

But perhaps the strangest thing was the absence of Hawthorne's diary. Hawthorne had been a dedicated note keeper. Prior to the trip to

Colorado, he had made several trips to the West, and with the assistance of his wife, had reported each of his adventures in exciting narratives that were widely read by a nation fascinated with the western wilderness. Each of his adventures except this one. The only record of this expedition left by Hawthorne was limited to some sketchy notes and a defensive letter written to his wife after he arrived in Santa Fe.

There were still many unanswered questions and David looked forward to talking with Fuller again. He was making notes when Fuller drove up.

"They're up there, all right," David said flipping a photo across the table to Fuller.

"So this is one of the campsites?" Fuller studied the photo. David handed him several others.

"Christmas Camp," David confirmed.

"Should be another one like this at the head of Pine Cone Creek," Fuller said without looking up from the photos."

"We didn't get over there. We got caught in a thunderstorm up on the ridge, and I thought that was it! What a noise! The rocks even hummed. And glowed."

"You were lucky you got down. You know what that humming and glowing means, don't you?"

"What?"

"That those rocks are charged, and they will draw the lightning just like a lightning rod."

"Well, it was some storm. It scared the horses off, and by the time we walked down we had lost interest in other camps. But I can show you where they are."

"I see you've been working," said Fuller pointing to the map on the table.

"I can't leave it alone."

"I know what you mean." Fuller sat down at the table with David and pointed out the site of the campsite at Pine Cone Creek.

"The Conejos Creek route is pretty convincing, isn't?"

"That certainly looks like the way they went up."

"Well, I think so. Did you get over there?"

"No, but we could see it from over the ridge. Do you think they came down the same way?" David asked.

"Probably. When they went up, perhaps they swung around the flank

of Varden Peak, along the 'bare ridge' referred to by Kirk, to the 'bowl-shaped summit' which was undoubtedly here." Fuller was pointing to the map. David sat beside him, leaning over the map. "The Christmas Camp was just over the ridge here where some of the stumps are. When they finally gave up and headed back down, they took 'the most direct route to the river', which would have been down this steep line here. There weren't enough men to carry what baggage they hadn't already abandoned, so they tried sliding it down here."

"That was a disaster," David volunteered.

"Right. It was much too steep so they had to retrace their steps and cross 'northeast over a low ridge', to this point at the head of Pine Cone Creek. Another of the camp sites is here. They probably followed Pine Cone Creek down to the valley." Fuller traced the creek.

"With all that baggage?" David said.

"With all that baggage," Fuller agreed. "That's what killed most of them. They were starving and exhausted, and struggling with that gear was simply too much for them. If they had left it and headed directly for the river they might have made it. Hawthorne has to take the blame for that."

"Hawthorne contended that he was giving the men a duty to try to keep up the men's morale," suggested David.

"Bad judgment."

"It certainly looks like they went up Conejos Creek, but why don't you think they could have been headed for Spring Creek Pass? I mean in the beginning? Look at this," David pulled the map to him and found the pass on the map. "Spring Creek Pass is a natural pass, and it is at the headwaters of the Rio Grande. It's only 10,000 feet the same as Coalbank Pass. That's not high at all for a Continental Divide pass. And look, it descends down this drainage to the Gunther and on out west to the Colorado."

"I suppose they could have been," Fuller said.

"Look at these." David went into the bedroom and returned with some large photographs which he arranged on the table.

"Satellite photos. Where did you get these?" Fuller asked.

"From the United States Geologic Survey. The National Cartographic Center. These are NASA high altitude aircraft photos. Spring Creek Pass is here. These two are the best ones. Manned space craft."

"Beautiful pictures. Sure shows Spring Creek Pass well." Fuller looked at the photos while David talked.

"Forsythe, a Taos trapper, said in his diary that he met Spanish priests there in 1820, just above Weminuche Gap. I'll bet the priests were using Spring Creek Pass. It would be the best shortcut from Santa Fe to the Gunther country and on out to California."

"No question about that. Maybe you're right. Maybe this is the pass at the headwaters that they were looking for, but they sure missed it. Conejos Creek is twenty miles north of that."

"Oh, well. I guess I'll give up on that one. I don't know how I would ever prove it. Maybe someday we will find Walker's diary."

"Now that would be a find," Fuller said, getting up and walking to the window.

"You know," he said, crossing his arms and leaning back against the wall, "I never have bought that story about Walker being killed by the Utes."

"You mean when Hawthorne sent him back to retrieve the cache they had buried in the mountains?" David asked.

"Ummm."

"That's what the Mexicans who went with Walker told the Army."

"I know. But why would the Utes kill Walker? Then that story about how they gave him a chief's burial. Why would they kill him and then give him a chief's burial?"

"Maybe they didn't recognize him," David suggested.

"They must have. He had lived with the Utes. He was adopted by them as a young man. He even had a Ute wife. And why didn't they kill the Mexicans ?"

"What are you getting at ?"

"Has it ever occurred to you," Fuller said, turning a chair and sitting in it backwards, "that Hawthorne might have wanted to make sure that Walker didn't live to tell his version of the expedition? Remember that entry in Kirk's diary? 'The greatest dread that Hawthorne has at the present is that a true and correct account of the proceedings above here may be made public'."

"You mean you think Hawthorne had Walker killed. Was it that important? You academic types are a cynical bunch."

"Hawthorne ran for president right after he got back, didn't he?"

"And would have won if he had carried Pennsylvania," David confirmed.

"It was bad enough that his expedition failed, that he didn't find a route for the railroad. He could blame that on Walker," Fuller continued.

"And he did," said David. "When he wrote to his wife from Santa Fe about the disaster, he said that his error was in hiring Walker in the first place."

"Exactly. But suppose it came out that Hawthorne had been responsible for the deaths of all those men. What kind of a chance do you think a leader with judgment like that would have had of being elected president? I'll tell you. Fat, slim, and none."

"Well, maybe that's a motive, but there's no real evidence that Hawthorne had Walker killed," David argued, "is there?"

"No, but it is an unusual coincidence, isn't it, that the only man who could have ruined him was murdered by 'Indians'?" Fuller placed emphasis on the word.

"You are cynical," said David. "If Hawthorne wanted Walker dead, why didn't Hawthorne kill him in the mountains?"

"Walker was an experienced mountain man. Indians and animals had tried to kill him almost every day of his adult life. I wouldn't think a man like that would be very easy to kill. Besides, Walker was no fool. He might have guessed that Hawthorne wanted to kill him. I'll bet he slept with one eye open."

"Maybe Hawthorne needed him?" David suggested. "Or maybe he thought Walker would die in the mountains and he wouldn't have to kill him?"

"Or maybe he didn't think of it 'til later?"

David walked over to the fireplace and stood poking at the fire.

"Ever heard of Moro?" Fuller continued.

"No."

"It's a little town east of Blanco. Near Taos," Fuller explained. "Was a rough place then. Still is. Had that reputation since it was settled by the Spaniards, was what they called an 'outlier.' It served as a buffer, to warn the Spanish at Santa Fe of Indian attacks. Any Indian attack would have come from the north. Since Moro was north of Santa Fe, it would have been attacked first."

"A trip-wire," David suggested.

"Something like that. Obviously no one wanted to live in Moro, so the

Spanish sent their convicts there. Rough bunch, even after the Spanish left and Moro became part of the United States. It was an isolated place so the people who lived there could do pretty much as they pleased. Moro was still a source of trouble when the army came to Santa Fe in the 1840s. There are plenty of records of that."

"And you think Hawthorne had someone, maybe from Moro, kill Walker?" David suggested.

"There might have been someone there who could be talked into killing a friend of the Utes," Fuller said sarcastically, "especially if he thought Walker could lead them to all that valuable equipment, too. "

"So," David postulated, "Hawthorne left for Santa Fe, left Walker behind to go retrieve the cache and then arranged for someone to kill him. Hawthorne had an alibi, and who would take the word of a Mexican outlaw from Moro over the distinguished James Hawthorne?"

"And the Mexicans got the cache," Fuller added and smiled.

David tilted the poker against the fireplace, leaned on one end of the mantle, and watched the blaze, thinking. It was almost noon. The September day was bright and sunny, but the fire felt good.

"I went to Moro this summer, before you came," Fuller continued, "to see what I could find out."

"And...?"

"I found out that they didn't want anything to do with this Anglo. I wanted to talk to the Alcalde or some of the old men about Hawthorne and Walker. Couldn't find anyone who could, or would, speak English, and my Spanish is pretty bad. Not much of a town. Ancient. The buildings and the streets are made out of the same mud. From what I hear, they don't like outsiders. Almost everyone in Moro belongs to the same family. There is one grandpapa for the whole town. "

"The don," David joked.

"The don. The godfather."

"A Mexican Mafia."

David walked back to the table, stood beside Fuller and looked at the map.

"I was thinking about going to Santa Fe," said David. "Just before I left New Hampshire, I went to the National Archives in Washington to look at the military records. The Army was functioning as the civil government in Santa Fe when Hawthorne came out of the mountains

after the disaster. I thought the army might have records of it."

"Good idea. What did you find?" Fuller asked.

"Nothing."

"Nothing at all?" Fuller turned in his chair toward David.

"Well, very little. I spent three days looking through the records and correspondence of the 9th Military Department and the Adjutant General's Office. The only mention of Hawthorne's party that I could find was a letter from a Colonel Munroe in Santa Fe to his commander in St. Louis. It was quoted by Dellen. I've got a copy of it here." David walked into the bedroom nearest the kitchen and returned with a single sheet of paper. He sat down by Fuller and read it aloud. The letter was written in the officer's handwriting and David traced it carefully as he read.

For the information of the Colonel...," David skipped ahead and continued. *"On my arrival I was informed that an American citizen was killed by the Utah Indians on the 21st of January. He was a member of Hawthorne's party who had gone into the mountains for the purpose of recovering some property left by the expedition. He was on the return, accompanied by eight Mexicans with the property when he was killed by the Indians. The Mexicans were released and one of them brought me the news of his death. He said six Indians came upon them as they sat by the fire. They were unsuspicious of any evil design and treated the Indians well. While they talked, one of the savages raised his rifle and fired, striking the man in the forehead. The Mexicans prepared to fly, but the Indians called to them and said they did not intend to harm them. The murderers, however, took possession of the mules and packs and ordered the Mexicans to remain where they were til dawn. I expect to mount a company on the morrow to investigate the matter and I will report to you all the information relative to the operation. I am respectfully, your obedient servant, J. L. Munroe, Major."*

Fuller picked up the letter from the table and re-read it to himself. He had not seen this letter before but had seen reference to it. "No follow up on this?" Fuller asked, handing the letter back to David.

"Not that I could find," David confirmed. "Seems funny, doesn't it, that the murder of an American citizen and the death of so many members of such a prominent public figure's expedition wouldn't have attracted more attention," David proposed.

"You would have thought so," Fuller agreed. "There may be something

in the State Archives or the Museum of New Mexico."

"Zip," David said flatly. "I wrote them. The archives and the museum said they had absolutely no material on Hawthorne or Walker. Suggested I check the National Archives."

"Complete circle," Fuller frowned.

"But I did have one other idea."

"Yeah?" Fuller was listening.

"The newspaper," David said victoriously. "The *Santa Fe Republican*. It has been published since January 1849, the year of Hawthorne's trip. It's the oldest newspaper in the West. When I was at the National Archives, I looked for old issues, but there weren't any. I did look at some of the newspapers they had. It wasn't an exhaustive search. I didn't have that much time, and looking at microfilm is so time-consuming and tiring. I looked at some old *New York Tribunes*, Greeley's paper, and the *St. Louis Republic*. But there were only second-hand reports and a few letters to the editor from travelers, but most of the information was sketchy, and a lot of it was wrong. I did find a book on New Mexico newspapers. That's where I found out about the *Santa Fe Republican*. I made it a point to try to check it out further when I was in Santa Fe next. I can't believe a newspaper would have overlooked that kind of excitement. That's why I want to go there."

"You're getting to be quite a historian, my friend," Fuller said.

David smiled at Fuller, folded his arms, and leaned back in his chair. "How would you like to accompany me to Santa Fe tomorrow on a little research trip? Maybe go by Moro again?"

"Can't think of anything I'd rather do."

FRIDAY, JANUARY 3

It has taken three days to move baggage only a mile – misery of these days difficult to describe – descent to the river proved to be demanding passage – ravines of perpendicular rock nearly level with snow many fallen trees – some inclines so steep the men fell often & slid uncontrollably with baggage 50-100 ft. – forced at times to crawl on elbows & knees pushing their bundles before them – men are in pitiful condition now – many with frozen fingers & feet - they have abandoned much of the baggage – it is all they can do to protect themselves from the cold – strips torn from their blankets wrapped around their feet for shoes must be thawed to be removed sometimes tearing away the soles of their feet in the process – what meat we had is gone – snow has driven off the game – if I could have imagined our plight we could have butchered mules & packed the meat down – even starving none has the strength now even to contemplate a trip back up the mountain for it – Mueller found few rosebuds & with these ate the last strips of parfleches boiling them to a poor broth or cooking them crisp on the fire – this afternoon Anderson his legs badly frozen lay down in the snow & begged to be shot – refused to go on – built a fire for him left some wood & blankets comforted him as much as we could – left him without turning our gaze back – courage of the men faded again after A's death – in spite of my best efforts they have split into quarreling groups – their condition is desperate.

8

The temperature in The Plaza was perfect. There was no wind and the bright morning sunshine just neutralized the September chill. David sat on one of the white iron benches across the street from the Governor's Palace, drinking coffee from a paper cup and reading a copy of the *Santa Fe New Mexican* . He had bought the paper from a boy wearing a green satin Notre Dame jacket and a bicycle helmet who stood in the middle of the street in front of the Palace selling papers to drivers when they stopped at the stop sign. Everyone seemed to know him.

Across the street from where David sat, in the long shadow under the Palace portal, the Indian traders had already gathered and sat against the wall in a mufti-line, silver jewelry and beads spread out carefully on colored blankets in front of them. Some of the Indians were old with traditional clothes and hairstyles. They sat back against the shaded wall, on aluminum folding chairs, blankets wrapped around their shoulders, silently watching the tourists who filed slowly by. Others, young men in Levi's and white shirts, and girls with purple sweatshirts, were more talkative, leaning forward on their knees, pointing out the advantages of their work to the squatting shoppers.

David was waiting for the museum to open at ten o'clock so he could look through the old newspaper files there, hoping to find reports of the Hawthorne expedition. He had driven down from Henson the afternoon before, crossing the Rio Grande first at Alamosa, and then again over the high canyon bridge at Taos, where he had stopped for chiles rellenos at Valdez's. It was one of his favorite places for Mexican food, and after two months of the enchiladas at the Pine Cone, he had made certain that he allowed enough time to stop there on the way down. The cheese was as good as he remembered.

David was glad, in a way, that Fuller had not been able to come with him to Santa Fe. He enjoyed the drive and it was nice having the country to himself. This gave him time to think and look without having to make conversation. There were some things he wanted to talk to Fuller about, but they could wait. He really didn't know Fuller well enough yet to spend that much time with him. You have to know somebody pretty well to travel with them he thought.

He wondered why Fuller wasn't still at the college, but he wasn't sure he should ask him about it. He didn't seem old enough to retire. David laughed to himself when he remembered that Dub had said the same thing to him. Maybe Fuller was sick? Maybe the college had asked him to leave?

It had been dark when David arrived in Santa Fe. In the clear night air, the amber lights of the town looked like a million topaz chips spilled across the hillside. As usual, he stayed at the La Fonda. The old hotel was on the plaza, near the museum, and he had always liked the dark lobby with the polished tile floor and the heavy furniture, even though in recent years it was getting crowded with tour ticket desks and people who wandered in off the street.

For breakfast he had green chile huevos rancheros in the coffee shop, then afterwards, found a bench in the sunny corner of the plaza with the pigeons, where he lounged feeling very self-satisfied.

The Plaza was a square block of closely-clipped grass, old cottonwoods, and brick walks. In the center of the plaza, where the walks met, was a monument to "those who fell in the defense of the frontier against the ——— Indians ." The adjective in front of *Indians* had been chipped away. The pink granite memorial was mounted on a circular wall just the right height for sitters who were already gathered on the east side of the circle sharing the sun. In another circle young people wearing hiking boots, flowered vests, large pieces of jewelry, tie-died shirts, and bandannas on their heads, played hackey-sack. A man played a pan flute. Pigeons walked about, were fed by lonely men, and were chased by a boy named Zakariah, who was urged by a mother in a green sweat suit and a toreador hat, not to. Curious couples with matching windbreakers and men with jogging suits and big stomachs came to look.

David liked almost everything about Santa Fe. He liked the bright wide space and the changing sky and the sunsets. The purple and rose-pink-rose of the summer cosmos and hollyhocks growing against adobe walls. The

singular blue window trim that keeps the evil spirits away. The rough, weathered grain of the chiseled wooden doors. The pungent piñon smoke. After New Hampshire he especially liked the sun and the dry air. He liked seeing the mountains from the town. He didn't want to be old, but he often found himself thinking of himself as an old man. He had noticed the older men and how they seemed to value warmth – and peace – and if growing old was to be inevitable, or possible, he had always thought this would be a good place for it. Old age seemed to last such a long time here.

He admired the Indian art work, particularly the old pawn jewelry, heavy silver and turquoise, the colored symmetry of the blankets and rugs, and the wonderful tactile satisfaction of the pottery. He enjoyed the sense of communion he felt with the past when he went to the stacked pueblos and the excavation sites. He felt stimulated by them and drawn to them in a way that was at once intellectual and yet oddly spiritual. The irresistible Anasazi mysteries fascinated him.

And then there was the food.

It had been a difficult choice for David, trying to decide whether he wanted to retire in Santa Fe as he and Susan had planned or try the mountain life in Henson. The altitude in Henson had worried him some, and he thought that with the cold weather and the isolation – you had to think about hospitals – it might be better to try Henson now before he got too old. Besides Santa Fe had always had a satisfyingly terminal feeling about it, and he could always save that for later. David was thinking about that when he heard the church bell ring.

David put the newspaper and the paper cup in the trash can, picked up his brief case and crossed the street. He made his way along the shaded Palace portal among the shoppers, trying to avoid the eyes of the Indians. He wanted to stop and look at some of the jewelry, he certainly had the time, but it always bothered him to look and not buy anything. It was like saying, "Sorry, this is not good enough," to a young mother or a student who had worked for months on a three-strand bead necklace or a sand-cast belt buckle. Susan had told him that everyone knew that the people who came to sell were not the ones who made the jewelry, but David wasn't sure he believed that.

He turned the corner at Washington Avenue and walked the two blocks to the museum. Cottonwood trees grew out of the brick walks and shaded both sides of the quiet street. The soft lines of the adobe buildings contrasted with the angular black shadows they cast on the pavement and in the doorways. David found the museum library, went inside and asked for Mr. Flores. A harried young man appeared and introduced himself.

"Yes," David had said when Flores had asked him if he could help, "I am doing some research on the Hawthorne expedition. I understand that you have a collection of New Mexico newspapers."

"Yes, we do," said Flores. "What are you looking for?"

"Well," David began, "I have a very specific request." Flores smiled patiently. Stupid thing to say, David thought. Everyone has a specific request. "I would like to see copies of the *Santa Fe Republican* from 1849. A James Hawthorne came through here in early 1849 after a disastrous mountain expedition, and I thought there might have been something in the papers about it."

"1849," Flores said, surprised. "I'm not sure we have issues back that far."

David opened his briefcase and took out the copy of *New Mexico Newspapers* he had brought with him, thumbed through it until he found the page he wanted, and put the book on the table so they both could see it.

"Here," David said, pointing.

Flores, still standing, bent over the book and read quietly, scanning the lines with his finger. "*Santa Fe Republican*. Weekly. English and Spanish. January 10, 1849 through December 24, 1852. Succeeded by the *Santa Fe New Mexican*, January 12, 1853 to present." He picked up the book. "Looks like we should have it. Come with me. I'll have to ask you to leave your briefcase here," he pointed to a wooden cabinet.

David put his case in the cabinet and followed Flores, who was still carrying the open book, down the hall. As he walked, he said over his shoulder to David, "Are you familiar with microfilm readers?"

David had used these at the National Archives. "Are they all alike?" he said.

"More or less," Flores said as he turned left into a small room. On a table were two readers similar to the ones David had used. On the wall to the left was a metal case, its shelves neatly lined with boxes of microfilm.

"This is the off-on switch," Flores began, standing beside the microfilm reader, "and this is the focus. Thread the film on these reels, the diagram is here. Find whatever you need in the case there. The boxes are arranged alphabetically by title and by year. Please, just take out one box at a time."

"Fine," David said.

"If you need any help, come and get me." He put the book down.

"Do you have a photocopier?" David asked.

"I can help you with that," he said. He placed his hands together. "All set?"

David thanked him and went to the case. He found the boxes of *Santa Fe Republican* tapes on the left end of the top shelf. January - July 1850, August-December 1850, January – July 1851, August – December 1851, January – July 1852. There was no box labeled January – December 1849. He looked again carefully, and then thinking it had been misfiled, looked through all the shelves. It was not there. He took down the box labeled January – December 1850 and spent thirty minutes reviewing the tape. The old papers were interesting, but as he had feared, there was no mention of Hawthorne or the expedition or Walker.

David walked out to the desk where Flores sat. "Can these boxes of film be checked out?" David asked.

"Oh my, no," said Flores seriously. "They are for reference only."

"Well," David said, "the tape I need is missing."

Flores looked surprised. "Missing? Maybe it's misfiled?" David didn't bother to tell him that he had thought of that. Together they walked back to the reading room and David stood behind Flores while the young man satisfied himself.

"Wait here just a minute," Flores said. Shortly he came back accompanied by an older man who seemed to be his supervisor.

"I'm sorry, Mr Walton," the older man apologized. "I'm afraid you have been misled. Our card catalogue does list the issues from 1849, but actually the oldest issues of *The Republican* we have are from 1850. We do not have the issues of *The Republican* you are looking for."

"But... " David began, picking up the reference book he had brought.

"Unfortunately, we have found many other mistakes in that book. Graduate students from the university compiled it. It was some sort of project. I'm afraid they weren't terribly accurate. This has come up before. *The Republican* is the oldest newspaper in the West, you know," the man said proudly. "We have had many requests. Many from collectors. Are you a collector?" he smiled.

"No," David said, impatient that the supervisor had changed the subject.

He's not taking me seriously, David thought. "Who else might have copies of those issues?" David asked.

"Do you mean which collectors?" The supervisor asked, patronizingly.

"I was thinking of which museums. Here or in Albuquerque," David said.

"If it is in the state, I can assure you, we would have it," the supervisor said. "No one else, no museum, that is, has a newspaper collection. The Archives gave us theirs years ago. There is an odd issue here and there, as you can see from this book, but none from 1849. There are no other collections that I know of. These are collectors' items, you know."

Great, David thought. Another dead end. Somehow he wasn't totally surprised. Just like the army records, he thought. The only records I need are the ones that are always missing. Now what? He could see his chances for his book slipping away.

He considered that as he walked back toward the Plaza. There was a big crowd of shoppers under the Palace portal now. Bored men with canes and cameras stood in the sun. Wash-and-wear women in windbreakers and sneakers, sunglasses hanging around their necks on little chains, studied the displayed jewelry. At the curb, several Indian cowboys stood by their pickup trucks talking.

"You don't suppose there is a collusion here?" David thought to himself as he walked. Walker, the only other survivor of the expedition, is killed supposedly by Indians who knew him. The army keeps no records. The only collection of local newspapers is missing the issues from that year. Wait 'til Fuller hears about this. Now he wished Fuller were here with him. He was a proper historian. Maybe he would have an idea.

David confirmed that the State Archives did not have a newspaper collection. Yes, they had given their collection to the New Mexico Museum, and they suggested he go there where they could surely help him. No, they were not aware of any local private collectors but suggested he check with some bookstores that handled rare books. The owner of the shop David chose said that no one he knew of dealt with old newspapers anymore. Too fragile. They deteriorate. Had he tried the museum?

Closed circle. He tried to think of other things Fuller would do, but nothing came to him.

It was noon. Nothing left to do but eat. The best bargain in the town was the Frito pie at Woolworth's, so he walked there. While he ate, he decided to go to Moro. But first he made a visit.

David drove out Alameda Street, along the river to the end of the pavement, then followed the sandy county road for three miles as it led winding up the hills from the stream. On top of the hill, set back from the road on five acres of chamisa and juniper and tufted grass was a one-story adobe house. The For Sale sign was still on the mailbox. Two large Russian olive trees shaded the walled patio that ran along the south side of the low house.

David parked in the drive and let himself in through the gate of the cedar post coyote fence that enclosed the small backyard, walling in the garage and the attached storeroom that he and Susan would have converted into a guest house. The grass in the little yard was uncut, and there were still no flowers in the beds they had planned along the fence.

He walked around to the front of the house, to the patio, and stepped over the low wall. He looked in the windows, and for a moment saw Susan reading in front of the kiva fireplace among the important things of their new life.

Then he walked back and sat on the low patio wall. There were mountain views in three directions. To the east, through the olive trees, the Sangre de Cristos. Down the valley, to the south, Sandia Peak near Albuquerque. To the west, the Jemez Mountains, three rows of hills, backlit by the sun, standing against the horizon like long scalloped boards, painted shades of blue and set on edge one behind the other.

David had dreamed of sitting in this patio in the sun, or lying in a hammock between the trees, or working with Susan on the flower beds along the adobe wall. Here he would have written his book. Here they would have had their sunny lunches, read their papers, taken their naps. Here they would have looked at the stars. Here they would have, piece by piece, built their new life, their new phase. Here they would have shared the sun and the space and the time. Here, but for a violent instant, they would have grown old.

The trip to Moro took an hour. It was pretty much as Fuller had described it. The village was quiet and very old. It looked deserted. The small doorways of the low adobe houses opened right onto the narrow dirt street that wound among them. Between the brown houses, barbed-wire-fenced vacant lots, shaded by cottonwoods and locust trees, were overgrown with chamisa draped with windblown papers like a primitive papier maché.

Thin, bored dogs walked in the streets in groups of three or four, or slept in the shade of pickups. Mobile homes with old tires on the roofs were parked askew under the trees. It was not the place you would like to have car trouble, David thought. Day or night. He glanced at the gas gauge.

At the west end of the little village, next to the church, was the general store, a cracked and fissured adobe building baked the color of gingerbread. It was also the gas station. In the shade of the portal, under one of the small windows, was a worn car seat and a coke machine. David knew without looking that under the machine's lift top, the bottles would be arranged in rows between silver metal dividers.

David stopped next to the first gas pump and got out. He stood by the car, not sure whether he should pump his own gas or wait. He didn't want to make a mistake. When no one appeared, he walked to the screen door. It was braced across the middle with a narrow aluminum Rainbo Bread sign. Little puffs of cotton plugged holes in the screen. When he reached to open the door, he was met by a man coming out. David backed out with him.

The man was Hispanic or Indian, David couldn't tell. He was stocky and short. He wore Levi's and a black Raiders sweatshirt. He had the body of a grown man, but his face was open and childlike, expectant. He stopped and looked at David, smiling, more curious than surprised.

"Gasoline?" David asked, as if he were talking to a savage.

"Hi," the boy-man said.

"Gasoline?" David asked again, pointing to the car.

Pause.

"How many dollars?" The short man asked seriously.

"Fill it up," David said. The boy looked puzzled. "Fill up the tank." David made a pouring gesture. The boy nodded and marched officiously to the car. He took the hose from the pump and hesitated, then walked back and forth around the back of the car, frowning, frustrated, carrying the hose in his hand. David showed him the gas cap behind the license plate. The man put the nozzle in the tank, squeezed the handle to start the pump, and looked up at David, smiling proudly.

David stood beside the car, leaned on the door, and watched the man. He's simple, David realized. "Are you the boss here?" he said to the boy, teasing.

"No," he said, as he nervously watched the spinning wheels on the pump. "My father's the boss. I put the gas in the cars."

An uncomfortable minute passed slowly. "I got this shirt in Albuquerque," the man said, thrusting out his chest so David could see it better.

David didn't know what to say. "It's a nice shirt." That seemed to please him.

"What's your name?" David asked, exploring. Fuller must have missed this one, he thought.

"Virgil," Virgil said quickly, standing up straighter.

"Virgil," David said, as if taking him into his confidence, "I'm looking for someone who might know about a famous man who came to this town a long time ago. A hundred years ago."

Virgil whistled softly.

"Have you ever heard of anything like that?"

Virgil thought about it. "The bishop from Santa Fe came here last year," he said proudly. Then after more thought, "My father might know this famous man. He knows many famous men. He knows Mr. Salazar. Do you know Mr. Salazar?"

"I don't think so," David said.

The pump snapped to a stop. Virgil removed the nozzle from the tank, replaced the gas cap, and hung the hose back on the pump. He studied the dials carefully. "Eighteen dollars and twenty," he announced, looking at David as if to say, "Can you believe it?"

Without thinking, David handed him a credit card. Virgil took the card, studied it carefully, then looked back up at David, confused.

"Eighteen dollars and twenty," he said again, still holding the card. David took the card from the mystified man's hands and replaced it with a twenty dollar bill.

When he finally returned with the change, David said to him, "Is your father here?"

"No," said Virgil.

"Maybe you could give this to him." Using the top of the car as a table, David wrote his name and address and phone number and the word "Hawthorne" on the card and handed it to the boy. Virgil looked at the card intently as he took it, then held it ceremoniously in front of him with both hands as David continued.

"I want to ask your father about this famous man. Maybe he could call me at my home or write me a letter if he knows anything about it." Virgil's face was trying to understand.

"It's on the card," David said patiently.

From the darkness behind the screen door a woman's voice, hasty, shrill, said something important in Spanish. Virgil, still holding the card before him, looked up at David. His eyes said good-bye. He turned and walked quickly into the store.

Well, who knows, David thought. Something may come of it. He started the car and drove away slowly. In the rearview mirror he could see Virgil and a woman standing in front of the store. They had been joined by a man who was watching David with binoculars.

9

"There has been an unfortunate coincidence," the man said, putting down the receiver and turning to face the other man. "Fuller has company."

"Anyone we know?"

"He is using the name David Walton. We are running that down now."

"Fuller went to Moro in June. Then Walton comes and asks for Fuller, and said he wants to talk to him about the expedition. Then, after they talk, Walton goes to Moro. I think the time we have feared has come."

A thousand miles away, Jose Cordova closed the door of his house and walked to his pickup. It wasn't yet light. He slid in and put his lunch kit on the seat beside him and started the old truck. In the valley he could see the lights of the little village. It was when he turned to back out of the yard that he realized that the gun rack was empty. The shotgun was gone.

David stood knee deep in the middle of the river below the pool, casting into the slick water above the riffles. The current sucked at his waders and made footing on the mossy rock bottom difficult. He had watched the shaded pool from the road and had seen large brown trout tailing there. Now he was trying to float a #12 Gray Hackle Yellow in a drag-free drift over one of the old fellows' noses.

He had fished the pool for half an hour and had caught three smaller browns, but couldn't seem to interest the grandpa. Leaning slightly into the current, he stripped the line into coils with his left hand, picked the line off the water cleanly into a backcast. "Bangor is a nice city," he had been taught to say as he waited for gentle tension that meant the line was straightening out over the water behind him. He pulled the spring-loaded rod down and forward, shooting the line from the loops he held in his left hand out through the rod guides. He watched the line as it formed a giant French curve. Just as the momentum of the shooting line was waning, he

stopped it with his left hand. The line straightened out over the water for an instant, and the the fly floated down softly onto the water just upstream from the log. Perfect, he thought. The fly bobbed for a few seconds as it drifted slowly past the end of the log. This is where the big brown would be, and he tensed slightly, expecting the strike any second. It did not come. The riffle at the tail of the pool snatched at the line, skating the fly quickly over the water and out of the pool. If he didn't like that, David thought, I can't please him.

He waded to the edge of the river planting one foot firmly before moving the other, reeling in his line as he made his way carefully through the swift water, angling slightly upstream against the current so it would not float him and push him down. He sat on the rocky bank, his feet still in the water, and took his lunch from the creel where he kept it.

He realized that it was almost noon, and that he had been fishing for three hours without thinking of another thing. Not the missing newspapers. Not the missing army records. Not Hawthorne. Not even the fact that Fuller would write the book he wanted to write. He had been totally absorbed with hunting the fish. He enjoyed reading the water for their likely hiding places, working quietly into a downstream position for the best casting angle, trying to drop the fly softly on the water just upstream from the target and letting it drift realistically by.

He ate a gooseliver sandwich and a Snickers, watched the river, and even though he wasn't supposed to, kneeled and drank the cold water. It was clear enough to see the sand grains on the bottom. He couldn't believe what he had heard about the risks of drinking from streams that beaver lived in, or that drained meadows where sheep grazed. He had never heard of anyone getting sick from drinking this water.

As he ate, he had watched an outsel, a little gray clown of a bird, hopping busily among the rocks and spray near the far side of the river. Occasionally the bird jumped into the water, submerged completely, to hunt for something on the bottom, then after a few seconds, popped back up on the rock.

David lay back on the smooth, polished rocks of the bank, watched the clouds, and listened to the regular music of the river. He and Susan had often spent the day along the river, she reading patiently or looking for flowers while he fished.

Then he walked along the bank further upstream, fishing some pocket

water, taking a few rainbow, and releasing them carefully from the barbless hooks. The river here below town – references to locations on the river were always based on the direction of flow – was wadable for miles, with a changing mix of pocket water, pools and broad slicks ideal for dry fly fishing. There were rainbow, brook trout, and browns, in the same river, depending on the type of water. Rainbow preferred the white frothy ripples of the faster water, the brook trout always the head of pools, and the brown trout, the slower water along the deep cut-banks and logs. David could predict what kind of fish would rise to the fly, and after the strike he could tell what fish he had on the line, even before he netted it. The rainbows were the jumpers, the browns fought stubbornly under the water like a dog on the other end of a stick.

The September fishing was always the best of the year. The water was low and clear and the big browns came up the river from the reservoir. David had always preferred catching rainbow because of their fight, their spirit. Their silvery sides looked cleaner and brighter than the dark browns that somehow seemed primitive, scowling, as if they had heard bad news or were keeping secrets that they learned in their deep pools. But in the fall, the browns did run bigger than the rainbow, some up to three or four pounds, and that increased the anticipation.

At this altitude, the river flowed noisily through spruce and pine woods and canyons. The spring run-off here was heavy and swift, and unlike eastern streams the rocky banks were wide, making it easier to cast without snagging the line in the willows and alders. Farther down stream, in the sage hills where the pitch of the land was less, the current slowed and the river was deeper, looping through grassy meadows where artificial grasshoppers would be deadly lures. Maybe he would go there tomorrow, he thought.

David spent the the afternoon moving slowly up the river, fishing the best looking water. As the shadows began to cover the river, making it difficult to see the fly on the surface of the water, he came to the old railroad bridge and realized that he had fished a mile above the car. He left the river and walked back down the road in the failing light. The familiar musk of the alders was pungent in the cool air, a smell as strong and as pleasant in his memory as the smell of rain on sun-warmed asphalt. What a way to spend the day he thought as he drove back to town. Trout live in such nice places.

After supper David sat for awhile on the porch of his cabin watching the

sky behind Crystal Peak go black. The stars appeared in their slow sequence, and in the clear high altitude sky they looked close, as if suspended by invisible strings.

He drank one Coors. Then one Olympia. Another dead heat. The night air cooled quickly and he went inside to sit by the fire. He tried to re-read some of the Kirk diaries he had copied, but the image of the man watching him with binoculars kept coming back to him and made him uneasy. The light inside the cabin made the windows completely black. He closed the curtains. Now he wished he hadn't left his name and address.

At half past nine, Fuller called.

"How was Santa Fe?" Fuller asked. "Sorry I missed it, but when sister says come, I come. I just got back. What did you find out at the museum?"

"You are not going to believe this," David responded.

"Try me."

"The 1849 issues of the newspaper are not at the museum. Issues from all the other years are there. Nothing from 1849."

"Why doesn't that surprise me?" Fuller said. "Did you try the archives?"

"They are not there either. The man at the archives said they gave what old issues they had to the museum several years ago. He couldn't remember if any issues from 1849 were included. You don't suppose there is some sort of..."

"Conspiracy?" Fuller finished his thought. "Another grassy knoll? Now you're the cynical one."

"I mean really," David said, exasperated. "It's all getting a little fishy, isn't it? An important expedition is decimated. One of the members is murdered under the nose of the army commander. The army takes little notice of it, or if it does, their records, if they kept any, are – well, let's say misplaced. An entire year's newspaper issues are missing. Too many coincidences for me." He paused to think. "Do you suppose collectors have them? If a collector has the newspapers, how could we reach him? Could we advertise? Is there a journal they read?"

Fuller smiled. "Well, maybe. But you're assuming that the collector would admit to a stranger that he had them. If someone did have those papers, it would not have been a legitimate purchase. You can be sure of that."

"You mean that someone would actually steal them from the museum?" David asked incredulously.

"Or buy them from someone who did," Fuller reminded him. "*The Santa Fe Republican* is the oldest newspaper in the West. The first year's issues would be quite a prize."

"But they would be worthless," David protested. "They could never be sold."

"Some collectors are funny that way," Fuller said. "Just having them is satisfaction enough, even if they can't be sold. Look at all the stolen paintings. It may not even be the money that interests them. There's no telling how many valuable documents and artifacts have been squirreled away. Things turn up after years and years in safes and attics when some of those collectors die." Then he continued. "Did you get to Moro?"

"Yes, I did," David said. "It was pretty much as you said. What a strange place. It was deserted. The only person I talked to was a fellow at the store, but I'm sure he was...," *simple* is what David wanted to say, "not quite bright. I didn't learn anything from him. I left my name and address with him and my phone number, but I doubt anything will come of that." He didn't tell Fuller about the man with the binoculars. Maybe we should talk to someone about Moro. An Hispanic. From what I can tell, an Anglo's going to get nowhere there, even if there is something to learn."

"Well," Fuller said, "I can't say that I'm surprised. Let's think about it some more. I'll give you a call in the morning."

Thirty minutes later, David was turning out the lights for bed when the phone rang. It was Fuller again.

"Guess what?" he said, and before David could answer, Fuller continued. "That old hermit was murdered. The one they call Buster who lived down by the falls."

"Murdered?" David said puzzled.

"Right. They found his body this morning. Apparently he had been dead two or three days."

"How'd you hear that?"

"Dallas came up. Told me when she was here just now. Said he was killed with a shotgun."

"With a shotgun?" David said. "Who would kill a hermit?"

"Nobody knows. Apparently no suspects so far, Dallas said. It sure wasn't a robbery."

"A murder in Henson," David said, mystified. "A real murder mystery."

"It gets better."

"What do you mean?"

"Buster's last name was Cordova."

"I don't get it," David said confused.

"The only people around here named Cordova live in Moro."

David and Fuller couldn't get close to Buster's cabin the next morning. Bright yellow strips of tape with POLICE LINES – DO NOT CROSS in bold black letters were woven through the trees. A few people walked around the outside of the taped perimeter looking through the trees at the cabin.

"Dallas said everyone in town was here yesterday morning when they took the body out," said Fuller.

People are funny, David thought. No one would wish anyone any harm, but when something happens, everyone wants to see it up close.

"Who would want to kill a hermit?"

"Beats me," Fuller said. "He never bothered anybody that I ever heard of. He's lived in that cabin for years. I don't think anyone knows very much about him."

"Tell me about the Cordova connection."

"Well, like I said, Cordova is not a common name. I never heard of anyone by that name who lived outside of Moro. No one there ever seems to move away. No one moves in. No one moves out. Some sociologists from the college even went there a few years ago to do some genealogy research, but they were thrown out. Or at least they couldn't get anywhere. That's when I first heard about the place."

"If Buster's name was Cordova and the Cordovas never leave Moro, what was he doing here?"

"I don't know," Fuller said. "Kinda' strange, isn't it?"

"You know what else is strange?"

"What's that?"

"The way he was killed. Shot in the chest with a shot gun? In his own place? Doesn't that seem strange to you?"

"It does, really."

"I mean, it's almost like..."

"An assassination?"

10

Jack Fuller had been one of the most popular history teachers at Rocky Mountain State College. He had several opportunities to go to larger schools, but as far as he was concerned, Rocky Mountain State was just the right size. And besides, he liked Gunther.

The little ranching town suited Fuller. It had everything he needed. There was a fly shop and a K-Mart, a Safeway and a savings bank, a drugstore and a Dairy Queen. The mountains were big and close. The population had been the same since the Civil War. The streets were wide enough to turn around in a wagon and traffic was light. Gunther wasn't on the way anywhere. You didn't get to Gunther by accident. Fuller and his environment had been a perfect fit.

He was an unlikely poet. At eighteen he had run away from home because he was tired of vaccinating cattle and digging post holes. He worked his way through college and graduate school and then lived for awhile in Denver, as he put it, "writing bad checks and blank verse."

When he had first taken the job in Gunther, Fuller had been stimulated by the theatrical excitement of teaching. He loved the performing. He wrote papers and articles and even a book, and for twenty years he thrived on the pleasant admiration of his students and peers. Then came "the accident," as he would call it. He had always referred to it as an accident, because it had come on him so unexpectedly, so suddenly. In retrospect, he should have seen it coming.

At thirty-one, going nowhere was just what Fuller thought he wanted. At fifty-one, going nowhere looked different. He grew stale in Gunther, but because of a haunting insecurity he was afraid to move on, or up, and that's what almost killed him. He became self-centered and withdrawn. He went to the mountains more often, but it didn't help. He drank more, at first to

feel good and then because he didn't. The writing stopped. He began to dread teaching because he couldn't summon the energy. He began to miss class. Weekends left him "wasted." On Christmas Eve, the dean, who had come to check on him and found him unconscious in his bloody vomit, probably saved his life.

He spent a year in the sanitarium in Pueblo. For two months Fuller didn't speak, and for awhile after that he would only say that he had been "to the top of the mountain."

The house in Capitol City had been his sister's idea and for awhile she had lived there with him. She still wrote to him, and occasionally she drove up from Delta to spend a few days. It was she who had met Dallas and asked her to look in on him.

In the beginning he had spent a lot of time fishing and walking in the mountains. His sister had made sure that his papers had been unpacked from storage, and she had helped him arrange his books. She thought it would be a way to re-establish the link, to help him take up where he had left off, and the doctors had agreed.

And it had helped him. While going through some of his old papers he had seen the Conejos Creek photographs again, and that reminded him of Hawthorne. In the the spring before David had come, Fuller had actually driven to Moro, but it wasn't until he had gotten David's card that he had thought about writing again. The card had bothered him at first. It was an intrusion. A threat. He resented it. He was afraid to call the number on the card and had left it on the table by the phone for two days. He was afraid that he would not have the energy for the obligation it might lead to. It was still easier and more pleasant to drift than to paddle. But when Dallas called, he decided impulsively to give it a try.

After the phone call from David, Fuller had spent the afternoon going back through some of his Hawthorne papers. His book on Hawthorne had started as a graduate school assignment to write a paper using original sources. It was in the 60s and John Kennedy had just been killed. Fuller had been struck by the parallels between the lives of John Kennedy and James Hawthorne. They were both sons of wealthy and politically powerful families. Both had a natural leader's charisma. Both were popular figures with distinguished military careers. Both had written extensively before their presidential campaigns. Both were attractive and ambitious.

Fuller had read everything he could find that Hawthorne had written – his diaries, the collection of his correspondence, the compelling narratives of his western adventures – and had been impressed with Hawthorne's energy, his determination, his skill as an explorer and a navigator.

From Hawthorne, Fuller had learned of the familial transfer of power. The legacy of power. He became interested in how families such as Hawthorne's could maintain their wealth and influence generation after generation, and even after 150 years could continue to exert a powerful unseen influence over American politics, banking, and diplomacy.

While he was teaching at the college, Fuller had the time to continue his research and to write. Publishing the book on Hawthorne had been a natural thing. The book was well received, attracting the academic attention he had hoped for. For awhile he had been invited to speak at symposiums and workshops. Editors of historical journals solicited articles. He was asked to review books. There was a certain momentum, and it energized him.

He remembered clearly the excitement when he had first recognized the sites on Conejos Creek, and how the realization had stimulated him to continue his research. He had gone to the creek and taken the photographs from the exact vantage points of the watercolors. He studied the maps and the diaries, recalculating the distances until he was sure. He even went back into the canyon in the winter to try to get a better feeling for the awful momentum of the disaster.

But the absence of Hawthorne's account of his last expedition continued to gnaw at him. Hawthorne was not the type of man to work silently. He craved attention and sought it. He could have easily rationalized the failure of his expedition. It was simply beyond his control. The weather was severe beyond imagination, the circumstances of survival so trying that failing meant dying. He was failed by the guide in whom he had placed his faith and on whom he depended. Under these conditions even the most skilled could become lost and did.

But there was no rationalization. Hawthorne didn't even try. No account of the adventure, however vaulting or self-serving, ever appeared. His correspondence did not deal with it further. It was as if the tragedy had never happened. After struggling down out of the mountains to Santa Fe, Hawthorne had left quickly for California where the Gold Rush made him a millionaire. He returned to Washington prosperous and stayed to become powerful, but he wrote nothing more.

In those academic days, Fuller had become such a fan of Hawthorne's that it was hard for him to see Hawthorne as anything but a heroic figure. He hadn't yet realized what he now knew Kirk had meant when he wrote in his diary that, "Hawthorne's greatest dread at present is that a true and correct account of the proceedings here in the mountains may be made public."

But now Fuller thought he understood. Driven by arrogance, ambition, and pride, Hawthorne had used the men of Moro to provide mankind's oldest instinctive solution for a problem that threatened to undo him, a preemptive attack, a desperate man's last defense against the blow he could not bear.

11

From the air the Antonio Valley looks like a giant thumbprint, sixty miles across at the base of the nail, as if someone had tried to pick up the state of Colorado while it was still soft. Surrounding the desert valley on three sides, mountains rise in a series of pointed whipped peaks, as if displaced upward by the pressure of the print in the formative gray meringue.

In the northeast corner of the valley, close along the slopes of the Sangre de Cristos, sand swept across the valley floor by the prevailing southwest winds has been deposited in dunes six miles long and 700 feet high. Through a fissure in the valley's western wall, the Rio Grande River, arising in the heavy snow pack of the San Juans, flows into the gravelly plain, makes a wide turn near Alamosa, and drops south like a plumb-line cutting a canyon a hundred feet deep in the alluvial debris on its way into New Mexico.

When James Hawthorne crossed the sand dunes and then the flat upper valley that unfortunate winter, he intersected an ancient thoroughfare passing up from the south and curving out through Coalbank Pass to the northwest, the route he should have taken, but for some reason did not. This trail, bearing along the eastern hillsides and longer than a more direct route across the valley, followed a topographical line marked by the scalloped junction of sagebrush and piñon. Buffalo wintering in the valley had used this trail to migrate to their summer range. Indians, linked in cultural tow, followed the buffalo in their seasonal circles. Spanish priests walked along it to California, and for the Taos trappers it was a shortcut to the beaver-rich valleys of the Green and White rivers.

But in time the old trail vanished. Except for a few short stretches recognizable in the spring as a lighter green in the new growth grass, the path has disappeared completely, as if carried away by the last travelers as they passed. The route the modern traveler takes south out of the valley is now blacktop.

It had been David's idea to go back to Santa Fe to look for more army records. "Maybe they were kept at Santa Fe and were never collected at the National Archives," he had suggested. Fuller was interested and asked to go along.

When they left Henson that morning, it was a crystalline fall day. In the clear air the mountains seemed close and oversized. They crossed the Divide at Spring Creek Pass and followed the Palisade Canyon of the Rio Grande into the Antonio Valley. At Alamosa they turned on U.S. 285 and drove south through the grass and farmland west of the river, between the Sangre de Cristos and the southern end of the San Juans. Passing just east of the rounded cone of Antonio Peak, the road rose along the highland flank of the San Juans, through the thick growth of pine and juniper.

Just beyond the highway town of Antonio, David pulled the car off the road onto a turnout overlooking the valley. The two men got out of the car, walked down through the trees and sat on the hillside. It smelled of hot pine. A noisy flock of blackbirds blew by overhead like a feathered squall.

From where they sat, the broad khaki grassland of the valley sloped away twenty miles to the east where it stopped against the blue wall of the Sangre de Cristos, stretching north and south as far as they could see. Here and there, spaced among the cloud shadows, isolated stands of cottonwoods shaded buildings the color of lions.

"Pretty nice, huh?" David said as they sat talking.

"Beautiful."

"You know, when I lived in Texas, I longed for water. For cool mountain air and moss. Then after all that time in New Hampshire, I began to miss this space. Life goes in phases and stages, doesn't it?"

"I guess the idea is to try to stay in phase," Fuller agreed.

"Flights to California come right over this valley."

David said. "I think the airlines must use Pueblo as a checkpoint. They come right over there," he pointed at Blanca Peak. "From the plane you can look right down on it. Once I caught on, I always asked for a window seat on the right going west, and on the left coming back east. In spite of all the time I spent looking at maps, I always learned something each time I flew over here. The distances look so much greater in real life than they do on maps."

"This valley is larger than Connecticut," Fuller said.

"I believe it."

"You have relatives in California?" Fuller asked.

"No," said David. "Most of my trips were for medical meetings."

"Will you miss medicine?"

David hadn't thought about medicine for months. He had been so preoccupied with his new life, so looking forward to it that he had almost forgotten where he had been one phase ago.

"In a way," David confessed. "I'll miss the patients. I enjoyed meeting them. And there are so many ways to help people now. I liked that. But it could be really draining. Seeing all that misfortune every day was depressing. Getting up for it got harder and harder. It's a performance in a way."

"Like teaching," Fuller observed.

"I guess so," David said. "But finally I just got tired." He didn't want to say he was burned-out. "And the hassle level got pretty high toward the end. There was so much third-party interference. There were so many unnecessary obstacles. It was like trying to drive with the emergency brake on."

"Sounds like the university," Fuller said laughing, his hand to his mouth.

"Well," said David, "that's behind us, isn't it?"

"Yep," Fuller said. "It's somebody else's turn."

David and Fuller sat for almost an hour on the hillside watching the sky and the changing light, talking about their careers and their lives. They enjoyed each other's company, but as men do, they talked only of events or told stories, avoiding anything

personal, or painful.

Back in the car, they drove on through the afternoon toward Santa Fe. Just past Ojo Caliente, the road dropped down off the hills into the sandy flat Chama River bottom. Directly ahead, a rainstorm had passed over the valley and the dark clouds were hung up on the mountains behind Santa Fe. A shaft of sunlight streamed under a low cloud bank behind them, brightening the pale grass in the foreground.

"Look at that sky," David said to Fuller. "You can't come out here without being taken with the sky. I guess that's one of the reasons I came back here."

"I know," said Fuller. "It's one of the reasons I've stayed."

In Santa Fe they took rooms at the La Fonda. There were no crowds. The next morning after breakfast, they walked the few blocks to the archives, down past the Plaza to Galisteo Street and across the bridge over the Santa Fe River. At the river they turned along the park. From there they could see Lake Peak over the pink and tan buildings of the city.

"Good morning," David said to the archivist, a deliberate, tidy young man with a bow tie. "I was in here last week looking for old newspapers." The archivist recognized him. "Now we are looking for any army records or correspondence you might have from the 1840's. The Ninth Military Command or the Second Dragoons." Fuller was impressed.

The archivist looked troubled. "I'm afraid," he said, thinking, "we don't have our material arranged topically. The records we have here were in private collections. If you could tell me a collection you are looking for..."

"I'm afraid I don't know any specific collection," David said looking at Fuller. "I have some of the officers' names. Would that be helpful?"

"Well, let's see. Come in here." The archivist led them into a small library. A large table nearly filled the room between the shelves. On the right-hand wall was a large card catalogue. "Let's see," he said again. He took the list of names David had given him and spent some time looking through the cards, frequently checking with the notes David had made.

"I'm afraid our listings don't include anything on these names, but the way the records are arranged, it's difficult to be sure." Then turning to them, frustrated, "Do you have any other information. Do you have the name of a collection?"

David looked at Fuller, hoping.

"I don't," Fuller confessed. "Maybe you could give us an idea where we might start? Do any of the collections include army records?"

"I'm not familiar with any," the man said, trying to be helpful. "Perhaps if you start with some of our larger local collections you could find something."

"It's worth a try," David said.

"Well," the librarian began, "I would suggest, let's see... Hitt's collection is a large one. And Blumenthal, and – let me check with Maria. She specializes in the period you are interested in."

He returned with Maria. Maria was an enthusiastic young woman with large dark eyes. She suggested two other collections.

"Here is how our files are arranged," the librarian said. "The collections are listed alphabetically by donor. The first card or cards contains the inventory of the collection which is complete, but sometimes there are many ways a document can be described, so check the dates." He looked at David, his face saying, "Do you understand?"

"Looks pretty straightforward," David said, looking at Fuller for agreement.

"You are welcome to use this room," the librarian continued, gesturing. "If there is anything I can get for you, let me know. I will check some of the other sources."

"Thank you," David and Fuller both said as they put their cases on the large table. They were the only two people in the room.

"Well," said Fuller, "you take these two at the front of the alphabet and I'll take these three."

For an hour the two men looked through inventories. Occasionally the archivist would bring them something to consider and seemed to be troubled when it was not helpful.

"He's really interested in this," David said.

"They are history junkies, too."

At one point the young man said, "What is it exactly you are looking for?"

"Well," began David, "in the winter of 1848, James Hawthorne led an expedition of thirty-three men on an attempt to find a central route for the railroad. They were stranded in the San Juan Mountains and all but Hawthorne and his guide died."

"Froze to death," Fuller added.

The archivist's eyes widened.

David continued. "Hawthorne and the guide survived and came through Santa Fe in January. When the guide went back into the mountains to retrieve some of the baggage they had abandoned, he was killed by Indians." David looked at Fuller. Why not say Indians, he thought. "The army was the only government here at the time." The archivist nodded in agreement. "And I thought army records or correspondence might contain some information about the expedition or the murder of the guide."

"Hmmm," said the young man, obviously interested. "Just a minute." He returned with Maria. "Maria says she has heard of the Hawthorne Expedition," he said, looking at David to make sure he had the name right. "In the winter of 1848?" he said to David, his eyebrows raised, seeking confirmation. Then he turned to Maria.

"Yes," she said thinking, "but only just the name. Was it an army expedition?"

"No," David answered, "it was privately financed, but I thought the army might have some records. I have looked at the National Archives, but there was nothing from the Santa Fe command."

"Have you tried the Bureau of Indian Affairs?" she said. David looked at Fuller. He hadn't thought of that.

"If the Indians were involved, the Bureau may have known about it. Maybe there is something there. Let me check," she said leaving the room.

David and Fuller were looking through some records when

she returned.

"I'm afraid this is all I can find now," she said, holding an old leather bound book. "Have you seen this? It is the official correspondence of James C. Calhoun who was the Indian Agent in Santa Fe from 1848 to 1852. Maybe there is something in here that will help." She put the book between them on the table. "I'll keep looking," she said, "and if I find anything else, I'll bring it out."

David and Fuller began looking through the book together. The letters were arranged chronologically. Excited by their new discovery, the two men skipped lunch and worked on through the afternoon.

"Look at this," David said. "It's from Calhoun to a Captain Judkins in Taos." He read softly:

I have been informed from various sources that articles of property which have been taken by the Eutaw Indians from an individual, a citizen of the United States, who was murdered by said Indians, have been purchased by certain Mexicans residing in the Moro. Notice is hereby given that all property of whatever description, whether mules, saddles, arms or clothing be delivered to you to be held by you until disposed of in proper authority. Individuals in whose possession such property may be found, and who fail to give notice of their holding it, will be regarded as having stolen it.

"That's where the story got started that the Indians did the killing," said David.

"The Mexicans told the army that the Indians were to blame."

"Look at this one!" David said excitedly.

Dear Sir,

This morning, I took a sergeant and proceeded to a village in the area and found the Villains with some of the clothing of the dead man. I arrested him and will keep him until you have arrived. The conduct of a great many of the Mexicans in the area is very suspicious. The prisoner informs me that the balance of the property belonging to the slain man is in their possession in the Moro. I await your instructions.

"Could this property be the baggage that Walker was returning with?"

"What's the date on that letter?" Fuller asked.

"March 10th," David answered.

"The timing would be about right, wouldn't it?"

Maria had returned and was standing beside the two men. "I'm afraid we have to close at five o'clock," she said. David and Fuller quickly turned and looked at the clock. It was 4:45. "You are welcome to leave your things here if you need to come back in the morning. They will be safe. We open at nine o'clock in the morning."

"I don't suppose," David said hopefully," that we could check this book out?"

"No," she said, confirming what he had thought, "it's against our policy."

"Do you have a copy machine we could use?" Fuller asked.

"Yes, it's there," she said, pointing, "but... "

"We'll hurry," Fuller said, picking up the book. In five minutes he had copied the pages they needed, one copy for each of them. They thanked Maria and left.

12

When the two men returned to the La Fonda, the lobby was filled with couples wearing cameras and practical shoes. David and Fuller had checked out of the hotel that morning, planning to return to Henson in the afternoon, but after spending all day at the archives, it was too late. They tried to get their rooms back, but two bus tours had arrived and all the rooms were taken.

For a while they sat in The Plaza, in the last of the sun, discussing their options. When it began to get cool, they walked down the street to the Inn of the Governors where they had dinner and stayed up until almost midnight, reading the letters and talking, excited about what they had learned.

The next morning after breakfast, they sat by the pool in the warm sun, re-reading the letters and making notes. The small pool area was deserted except for a large woman with a pained expression reading *The Firm,* and a muscular young man who stood in the sun, inspecting his body for flaws.

David read to Fuller. "Listen to this letter."

Having heard from a source considered to be reliable that a considerable amount of the property belonging to the American guide killed in Apache Pass is now concealed in some of the houses in the Moro, I respectfully request that you take a detachment of men and proceed to that point and make a strict search for the same. Should you find any portion of the property, kindly bring the same to this office together with the person or persons in whose possession it is found.

Your Obedient Servant,
James Calhoun"

"If the Mexicans had the clothes, it certainly makes them suspect, doesn't it," Fuller said.

"But the Mexicans said they ran away after Walker was killed," David said, "and that they got the clothes from the Indians."

"I'm not sure the army bought that completely, at least from the sound of some of these other letters from Calhoun."

"Well," said David, "it sounds as if the baggage did end up in Moro. That means that Walker had found the cache and was headed back here with it."

"Here or somewhere," Fuller emphasized.

"And you think that after Walker found the cache, the Mexicans killed Walker, took the baggage and told the army that the Indians did it?" David tested.

"That's my guess," Fuller confirmed. "The Mexicans may have followed him, waiting for him to find the cache and then ambushed him."

David thought about Fuller's idea. He admired Fuller's confidence. Maybe he was right about the Mexicans, David thought. He was right about Conejos Creek. The photos pretty much settled that.

"This letter," David said," says that Walker was killed in Apache Pass. Where is Apache Pass?"

"I've never heard of it," Fuller said. "I always thought Walker was killed somewhere along the Rio Grande. A pass suggests that he was in the mountains somewhere. There are no mountains between where they left the cache and Santa Fe."

David was thinking. "We need a local expert."

"How about Maria, at the archives," Fuller suggested. "If anyone around here knows, I'll bet she does."

They walked the few blocks to the archives and looked up Maria.

"Apache Pass," Maria said looking puzzled. "I've never heard of it. Not unless it's near Apache Mountain." She walked to a large wall map. "Here," she said pointing, "just south of Santa Fe." She seemed happy to be helpful.

"That's too far south," Fuller said. "The Apache Pass we're looking for would have to be north or east of Santa Fe."

"Bill," she said, walking back into his office, "have you ever heard of Apache Pass?"

Bill came out of the office with her, thinking. "No, but," he walked to a bookshelf, found the book he wanted and put it on the table in front of them. "The *Atlas of New Mexico Place Names*," he said, turning the pages. "Maybe Apache Pass is here. Yes. Here it is." He read, "Apache Pass. Taos County. Now called Red River Pass. Route of state highway 38. Summit 9200 feet. Open year round." He looked up.

The three men were pleased. Maria was concerned.

"But, Bill, that's all Ute country. The Apaches were out on the plains, here," she noted, pointing to the map again. "The Apaches and the Utes didn't get along. It seems a funny place for an Apache name. It's not a name an Indian would have given it. Whites must have named it Apache Pass, for some reason."

"You have been very helpful," Fuller said to Bill and to Maria, who still looked a little troubled.

"It's our pleasure," Bill said. "Anything else you need?"

"Just a little time to assimilate all this." David and Fuller walked into the library and spread out a map on the table.

"Let's see," Fuller said, leaning over the map, "Walker was killed after he found the cache, right?"

"That's what the army letter said."

"On the way back to Santa Fe, or somewhere," Fuller said, building a case.

"Right."

"Then look at this," Fuller said to David, "Apache Pass is north of Santa Fe. It's north of Taos. It's not on the way to Santa Fe. If Walker was bringing the baggage back to Santa Fe to forward to Hawthorne, what was he doing way over here?"

David was leaning over Fuller's shoulder. "Maybe," he suggested, "if the Mexicans really did kill him, they kidnapped him and took him into the mountains to kill him."

Fuller continued. "Look at this. If you take Red River Pass – or Apache Pass – east, you would come out here at Cimarron. It's only about thirty miles." Fuller straightened up.

"And?" David asked.

"Cimarron is on the old Santa Fe trail."

David looked at the map. "But that's way out of the way."

"Unless you're going to St. Louis," Fuller suggested.

"You mean...," David began.

"He was on the lam," Fuller said, smiling.

"With the baggage," David said.

"With the baggage," Fuller confirmed.

"So he was stealing the baggage, just as you said."

"Sure looks like it, doesn't it?"

"Look at this," said Fuller, who had bent to look at the map again. "Apache Pass is very near Moro." They stood looking at the map.

"So," began David, "Walker returns for the baggage and finds it. Instead of returning to Santa Fe, he cuts across the mountains, bypassing Taos, and heads for the Santa Fe trail and maybe St. Louis. At Apache Pass he is killed by the Mexicans who take the baggage and tell the army that the Indians did it."

"It would fit, wouldn't it?"

"And you think that Hawthorne put them up to it?" David asked.

"It certainly would have been in his interest, wouldn't it? Suppose Walker had returned to Santa Fe – or St. Louis – with the story that Hawthorne had ignored his advice, bungled the expedition, got them all lost in the mountains and was responsible for the deaths of thirty-three men?"

"That's going to be tough to prove, isn't it?"

"Maybe," said Fuller, "but we've already learned much more than I thought we would. Who knows?"

Fuller looked at the map for a while, then sat down and crossed his arms as if completing a task. "You and I need to take a trip," he said, smiling at David.

"To Apache Pass?" David asked.

"To Apache Pass."

13

"You can see the track of the Trapper's Trail there," said Fuller. The two men were standing on one of the rocky juniper ridges that slope off the backbone of the Sangre de Cristos like a series of ribs. Between the ridges were long triangular water courses, their apexes pointed up the mountainside. It was to a line along the side of the mountain connecting the upper ends of these water courses that Fuller was pointing.

"The old trail followed that line, there" he continued, "just above the head of these ridges, just at the edge of the piñon. Travel was easier there than continually going up and down the ridges. The elevation up on the side of the hill made it easy for them to see out over the valley and the piñon provided cover and firewood."

Below the ridge where they were standing, the Rio Grande Valley, dotted with juniper and their long shadows, stretched north for another fifty miles. It was perfectly level except for three black cinder cones that sat like pieces on a game board. Through the length of the valley, about where the game board would fold, the river had cut a jagged, shadowed canyon. To the west, beyond the morning pastels of the valley, the San Juan Mountains were fully lit by the sun.

"See that old building?" Fuller was pointing down into the narrow canyon nearest them. There next to a small stream, were the crumbled, rectangular remains of an old rock foundation. "That's Turley's Mill," he said. "Home of the famous Taos Lightning. It was a hotel also. The stables were there, and that's the field where Turley grew the grain to make the mash. That old wheel provided the water power. And it was no accident that Turley built his mill right on the Trapper's Trail."

David laughed. "A nineteenth century convenience store."

"He got them coming and going," Fuller said. "Six months after the

annexation of New Mexico a group of Mexican nationalists and Indians sacked Taos and then came up here to burn out the Americans who had fled to the mill."

What a violent life those people led, David thought, studying the old mill site.

"From here," Fuller continued," the old trail ran north, along the Sangre de Cristos, across the Antonio Valley north of the dunes and crossed the Divide at Coalbank Pass."

"Too bad Hawthorne didn't take that trail, "David said. "If he had, there might have been a railroad in California fifteen years sooner."

"We're going along that highway there," Fuller said. "It parallels the old trail. At Red River we will turn east through the pass." Now he was pointing to a map. "Here is Cimarron and here is the route of the old Santa Fe Trail." He indicated a line up from Santa Fe north to Raton.

"But why cross Red River Pass to the Santa Fe trail?" David said. "Why not go due west from the river and cross the mountains at La Veta Pass?"

"Too far north," Fuller said. "It was still winter in March, and I doubt Walker was in the mood for any more snow."

They stood looking at the map unfolded on the hood of the car.

"And here is Moro," David said. "Right on the route to the Santa Fe Trail."

"Let's go see what we can find out."

Red River Pass is not a high pass. Following the narrow river canyon upstream, it crosses the Sangre de Cristos well below timberline. Beyond the summit, the land falls away to the east in a series of broad valleys and round hills dotted with piñon stubble like great whiskered faces. On the east side of the pass it is much drier, typical of the Rockies at this latitude, where the moisture in the prevailing westerlies condenses out quickly as they are drawn up the western slope. The pine trees, even near the summit, are widely spaced, especially on the sunny south-facing slopes. What green there is in the valleys closely borders the streams where there is grass and alders.

Coming down from the summit of the pass they could see beyond the valleys where the hills flattened out against the plains. There braided lines of cottonwoods marked the last of the water and the site of Cimarron. It was noon when they arrived.

In the four-square plat of the little town, the buildings were widely

spaced along broad dirt streets that ran the direction of compass points. Large cottonwoods grew in a dusty park across the street from a row of one-story buildings.

They drove around the empty park and stopped in front of the only store that seemed to be open. One jeep was parked in front of the light brown stucco buildings. On either side of the door there were large storefront windows. In the left hand window, a small black and red hardware store sign announced, "Yes, we're Open." In the right window was a hand-lettered, "Welcome." Over the door a sign identified the building as the "Art Gallery and Malt Shop."

"How can you resist a combination like that?" David asked.

Inside the store it was cool and smelled of floor polish. An antique soda fountain ran along the left wall near the front door. On a wood and glass showcase across the room was the cash register. The rear of the store was lined on both walls with paintings of what appeared to be local scenes, and in the middle of the room, mismatched tables were crowded with gifts – little cedar boxes, rock collections, pottery, kachina dolls.

"Hello." The voice belonged to a large man limping toward them from the rear of the store. His stomach strained the buttons of his checked shirt and protruded over his belt, almost completely hiding the turquoise buckle.

"Morning," Fuller said. David nodded.

"What can I do for you fellows?" the man asked.

"We are doing some research," Fuller began, as the man walked around behind the showcase between them, "and we're looking for Apache Pass."

The man looked at them, unable to conceal his suspicion for a couple of nosey strangers doing research. Then after thinking it over he said, "That's the old name for Red River Pass, I think."

Fuller was unfolding a map on the counter between them. "This area?" Fuller asked.

The man turned his head slightly to see the map better, studied the map for a minute, and pointed. "Yes. See just west of us." Then he straightened up.

"Was this a pass in the 1850s?" Fuller seemed to be doing all right so David decided to let him do the talking.

"I think so," the man said. "My wife here's the one who knows this country the best. She was raised here." His wife had quietly joined them,

interested to see who these strangers were and why they were talking and not buying.

"This is my wife," he said, turning to the tanned woman. "These fellows are looking for Apache Pass. Wasn't that the old name for Red River Pass?"

"Well," she said, "the road takes a different route now, but that's what they used to call it. Did you come in over highway 38?" she said to Fuller.

"Yes," Fuller confirmed.

"Then you came right down it most of the way. The old road branches off about half-way down the pass."

"Would that have been a pass in the 1850s?" Fuller asked again.

"Yes," said the woman, "it was an alternate route to the Taos Valley and Santa Fe. Didn't have to go all the way down to Wagon Mound and around."

"Why was it called Apache Pass?" Fuller asked. "Wasn't this all Ute country?"

"Well," the woman said, warming up, "it was, but the Jicarillas had an agreement with the Utes . They let the Utes come out on the plains to hunt buffalo, and Utes let the Apaches come up the valley to gather willows. For baskets," she added before Fuller could ask. "The early settlers here called it Apache Pass." She turned to her husband. "I haven't heard Apache Pass in years."

"Can we get up there?" Fuller asked.

"It's all private land now," she said frowning. "Part of the Wheeler Ranch. They keep the gate locked. We used to go up there for picnics when we were kids." She paused trying to decide whether or not to ask. "What do you want to know about Apache Pass?"

"An old guide was supposed to have been killed by the Indians there," Fuller said. "We just wanted to look around some."

"Bill Walker," the wife said.

"That's right," Fuller said, looking at David. "You know about Bill Walker?"

"He was all over this country," she said. "He was one of the Taos Trappers." The husband smiled proudly.

"Well," Fuller began, not sure how to proceed. "If he was using that pass, where might he have been headed?"

"Darned if I know," said the wife. "If he was coming this way he was probably cutting across from the Taos Valley to 'the Trail.' The Santa Fe Trail," she specified. "It ran right through here, you know."

"Yes," said Fuller.

"If these fellows are interested in Bill Walker," she said, turning to her husband, "they should talk with Ruth." The husband nodded. "Ruth Winchell," she said to Fuller by way of explanation. "She really knows the history of this country. Too bad she is away or you could go up and see her today."

"Away?" asked Fuller.

"She's gone to Denver to visit her son, but she'd be the one to talk to. She's eighty-seven years old. Knows all about this country. She's lived here all of her life." Then she added, "You going to be here long?"

"Actually, we just came over for the day," Fuller said, "but maybe we could come back." David and Fuller nodded at each other.

The husband had made his way across the room and stood behind the soda fountain, rearranging glasses.

"How could we get in touch with her?" Fuller asked.

"Well, she can't see to read, and she refuses to talk on the phone. I don't think she can hear well enough. She lives right at the edge of town. You came right by her place. It's the old stone house set back from the road, just across from the volunteer fire department. You can see it from here." She and Fuller and David walked to the window. "There," she said. "The tin roof."

"Well," said Fuller, "you have been very helpful. We will have to try to get back and talk to her."

"It's my pleasure," she said, smiling. "We don't get many researchers here. Where do you live?" she asked Fuller.

"In Henson. Colorado."

"Tell you what I can do," she continued. "You put your name and number on this card," she handed him a card, "and when I see her next week I'll tell her you were here and what you wanted. I think she will probably be happy to talk to you about it."

Fuller took his pen from his pocket and wrote on the card the woman had handed him while she watched. She took the card, and with a deliberate ring, opened the register and put the card in the cash drawer.

"This is our store pamphlet," she explained, handing Fuller a brochure from a stack on the countertop. "The phone number is on it. If you call and tell me when you want to come, I'll tell her." Fuller tucked it in his pocket.

"You stop that, Weston!" The woman said across the room to her husband, who was smothering a smile. Then turning to Fuller, "Excuse my husband," she said. "He's being rude."

"You gonna' tell them Mrs. Winchell is," Weston paused to think of the right word, "about half a bubble off plumb?"

"Never mind him," she said directing her warning to her husband, "he thinks anyone who is different from him is off their beam." And then to Fuller. "Ruth Winchell is an old lady, and old people sometimes do things a little different. You will like her, and she can tell you what you want to know."

David, obviously pleased with the progress Fuller was making, had wandered over to the soda fountain and sat on a stool.

"How about a malt?" he said across the room to Fuller.

"Buy one and get one free," Weston said, smiling expectantly.

"Good luck with your research," the woman said, walking toward the back of the store.

"Thanks again. We'll stop by and let you know what we have learned."

She waved without turning and walked through a door in the rear of the store and was gone.

"What flavor?" Weston asked, holding two tall glasses.

"It's got to be chocolate," David said spinning around on the stool to face him.

"Two chocolate malts," Fuller confirmed, taking a stool beside David.

Weston turned to work while David and Fuller watched. He carefully carved the ice cream from a tub in the top loading freezer, scraped it into the tall metal malt cups, methodically added the milk, and then finally clicked two measures of malt from the dispenser into each cup.

"You know," David said to Fuller, "malts are one of the things I missed most about the West. Thunderstorms and malts."

Weston studied the cups, decided that he had the mixture right, and snapped the cups, one at a time up into the green metal mixer. He flipped the switch and watched as the mixer whirred.

"No malts in New Hampshire?" Fuller asked.

"Milk shakes," David said, "and something they call frappés, but no malts."

"What's a frappé?" Fuller asked.

"Just a thick milk shake, best I could tell. Not even close to a malt. Not near as thick. There's not as much ice cream as a malt."

The whirring stopped. Weston inspected both malt cups, and then apparently satisfied, poured the thick mix slowly into tall soda glasses. He set the glasses deliberately in front of David and Fuller, put the frosted metal cups beside each glass and stood back, obviously pleased with himself.

"There," he said, handing them straws. "Two chocolate malts." David toasted Fuller with the full glass.

"Oh," said Weston absentmindedly. He turned to the counter and handed them each a spoon. "You'll need these," he beamed.

JANUARY 6

Storms again – compelled to stay this camp two days – most miserable days yet – impossible to describe unless experienced – nine died yesterday – J raved all night had violent fit & fell headlong into fire never recovered – F died this AM – H soon after – S wandered off & has not returned – unbearable craving for food & salt – shared two tallow candles this AM – last PM found old bones in our cave wolf den pounded them to pieces & boiled with last of rawhide laces. Try to move again tomorrow.

14

The next week passed slowly for David. It was exciting to think that Mrs. Winchell might know something more about Walker's death, and he was looking forward to talking with her when she returned. Maybe she could even support Fuller's idea that Hawthorne had Walker killed.

From the Indian Agent's letters, it seemed possible that the Mexicans had done the killing. There certainly seemed to be a lot of suspicion of that at the time. But establishing a link to Hawthorne? David couldn't see how that could be done after all this time. And what if some link could be established? Could it be revealed? Was it a story that could be told? Would telling it be defamation of Hawthorne's character? It was pretty clear how the Hawthorne family would react to the slandering of one of their most famous relatives. They would probably sue anyone who made such a suggestion. And anyway, a motive didn't make a murder. But still, it was worth knowing.

David sat in the kitchen looking at the map spread out on the table. In red he had marked the route of the expedition across the Sangre de Cristos into the Antonio Valley, northwest toward Coalbank Pass to the turn – the inexplicable turn – then southwest to Conejos Creek. The red line wiggled up the creek to the south ridge of Varden Peak where a red X marked the site of Christmas Camp. A green line was traced over the retreat, back over the ridge, past the green X that marked the site of the Pine Cone Creek Camp, down Pine Cone Creek to the valley. From the mouth of Pine Cone Creek to Blanco, he had drawn a dashed line, roughly paralleling the Rio Grande as it bent east across the valley then turned south, but since the diary entries had stopped before they left the mountains, the exact route Hawthorne and Walker had taken back

across the plains wasn't known. David only presumed that the two survivors would have kept to the timber along the river for firewood and what little protection the trees offered against the winter and the wind.

David tried to imagine what it must have been like those January days and nights, walking fifty miles across deserted country, hungry and freezing. In New Hampshire he had seen hypothermic, homeless men brought into the emergency room, barely alive, cold and stiff, unable to speak or move, their staring sightless eyes fixed on something horrible far away. How could Hawthorne and Walker have summoned the energy to survive, especially after what they had already been through?

David had been in real physical danger only once. He had fallen out of a canoe in New Hampshire in November. His life vest was old, and it and his heavy wool clothes had become quickly soaked with the icy river water. He was shocked by the cold water, but since he could swim, he was not frightened. For the first few minutes, by frog kicking and using the paddle he had instinctively taken overboard with him, he was just able to keep his face above the water. But even struggling, he found he could not force his way out of the deep eddy where the current had trapped him. Somehow he made it to the edge of the eddy where the faster current caught him and swept him into the mainstream of the river. He had only been in the water for a few minutes, but when he washed up on a gravel bar, he could not stand. He could not make his muscles move. He shivered for hours afterward, so violently that he splashed water out of the tub his friends had put him in to warm him. He did not realize until later how near death he had been.

He looked back at the map on the table. A yellow line drawn from Blanco down to Santa Fe and then west was Hawthorne's route to California.

The blue line was for Walker. From Blanco, it led back along the river to Conejos Creek and the site of the cache. When he first drew the blue line, it stopped there. Later he added the return, back down the river to Apache Pass where there was now a blue X.

The authority of the colored lines made it all seem so clear. There was, after all, some evidence that the colored lines marked the actual routes. There were the diaries, the watercolors, the campsites, and Hawthorne's letter to his wife, written or apparently written, from

Santa Fe.

But the blue line was the troublesome one. Was Walker stealing the baggage as Fuller had suggested, David thought. At sixty-two, Walker must have known that his trapping days were over. When Hawthorne had found him that fatal autumn, Walker was living with some other trappers and a few Indians in a miserable adobe fort on the Arkansas River. He was still nursing a bullet wound he had received the summer before. And yet he had reluctantly agreed to guide Hawthorne through the mountains, even though others had refused because the cold upon the mountains was unprecedented and the snow deeper for that time of year than anyone had ever seen. According to the Kirk diaries, Walker had said that he thought it was possible to get through the mountains, but then in an ominous addition he added "though not without considerable suffering."

Maybe Walker needed the money. As a trapper, even a good one, he would have made only $150 in a good year. Maybe he couldn't resist the call of adventure that for forty years had been his life. Maybe at his age he felt time slipping away, mocking him. Whatever the reason, the strength of it drove him at age sixty-two and with one lame arm to head off against his better judgment with Hawthorne into a winter that promised to be the worst he had ever known.

Was Walker a thief? His reputation was certainly checkered. To some he was vicious and dangerous. His drunken sprees were renowned, the stuff of legends. On one occasion he had taken the furs of his Indian friends to Taos where he sold them and spent the money on whiskey and bolts of calico that he drunkenly unfurled in the windy streets.

Perhaps Fuller's suggestion wasn't that-far fetched. Walker certainly could have found his way to the Santa Fe Trail and from there disappeared with the baggage he had salvaged. The money he could have made from selling the baggage – estimated to be worth ten thousand 1850 dollars – would have likely been more money than he had earned in all his life. Maybe he did try to buy off the Mexicans. It was becoming easier to believe.

While they waited in Henson for Mrs. Winchell to return to her home in Cimarron, David and Fuller had spent their days fishing together. Sometimes in the mornings, just after sun up, they went to the river below town to fish the deep-shaded pools for brown that had come up from the reservoir. Or they went to Acme Creek, near Fuller's place, to fish the swift riffles and pocket water for rainbow. One afternoon they went down to the meadows, just above where the West Fork joins the main river. Here in the flat valley, the speed of the water slowed and the rocky banks of the upper river were replaced by broad winding channels cut in the grassy banks. Wading the waist-deep water, the two men fished in turns, each casting until he got a strike, then stepping back for the other to take a turn. This doubled the excitement.

David watched intently as Fuller cast the artificial grasshopper, bouncing it expertly off the banks to fall motionless on the water, and then if that produced no strike, jerking it slightly as it drifted, as if it were struggling on the water. When the action slowed, Fuller changed his casts, splashing the hopper down heavily on the water – something fishermen instinctively avoided, for fear of spooking the fish. But often these splashes were met with an immediate strike. David was a good flycaster, but he was learning from Fuller.

"Ever seen a live hopper land in the water?" Fuller said. "It looks like a plane crash. Fish know that," he said, continuing to cast. "It's the way they make their living. If you put a Grey Hackle yellow or a mosquito down like that you're wasting your time. But hoppers – watch this." He flipped a cast toward a cut bank thirty feet upstream where a large brown had been rising, dropping the rod tip down almost to the water as he cast, ensuring a heavy landing. A fish slashed at the fly almost instantly, but the line came back limp. Fuller quickly cast again, sending the hopper to the same spot. The fish struck again, and Fuller's rod bowed.

"When they're hitting, they're hitting," Fuller said smiling as he played the fish. "Works every time. You'd think it would scare them off, spooky as they are sometimes, but putting it right back after a strike almost never fails." Fuller released the fish and David took his turn. They alternated up the river, fishing until it was too dark to see the fly, setting the hook when they heard the fish strike.

After dark the two men sat on the bank, talking and looking at the stars.

"When I was a kid, we used to come here to Henson every summer to fish. With three other families. The men fished together every day.

It must have been like this. In those days there weren't so many fishermen. Henson hadn't been discovered, I guess. My father was a doctor, and somehow everyone found out when there was a doctor in town. In the evenings sheepish men came by the cabin to ask my father to remove the flies they had accidently hooked in their ears. Sometimes they hooked their ears with a fly, and if fishing was really good, they would just cut the leader and leave the fly in their ear 'til they finished for the day. I remember one night, this man came by with a fly in each ear! He had hooked one ear, cut off the fly and later hooked the other ear. Then he cut that fly off and kept fishing, a fly hooked in each ear."

"Must have been some spot," Fuller said.

"Must have been. I remember hearing my father tell the man that he wouldn't charge him to take the flies out of his ears if he would tell him where he had been fishing."

Fuller laughed, his hand to his mouth.

"When I was living in New Hampshire, I had a dermatologist friend who had grown up in Arizona. He and I used to talk about the sky, and what a big part of our lives it was for us as kids. How we were always so aware of it. We both had the same memories of summer nights. Our parents would have company over and we would all go out in the backyard, maybe because it was hot. There was always watermelon, or homemade ice cream. The adults sat in lawn chairs and talked or told stories. The kids lay on the grass on quilts, listening and looking up at the stars. We knew all the constellations and the brightest stars. We counted shooting stars and lightning bugs. One of my most pleasant memories is drifting off to sleep under that huge sky with my parents and the stars close enough to touch."

"Hard to imagine 'til you've seen it," Fuller agreed.

"My kids grew up in New Hampshire," David said. "It wasn't the same for them. Maybe because we didn't sit out in the evenings. The mosquitoes and black flies were bad 'til September. Maybe the sky wasn't so clear."

"Maybe the times have changed," suggested Fuller.

The two men talked and told stories for another hour. On the way home, reluctant for the day to end, they stopped at the Pine Cone for enchiladas.

Saturday night it rained. The run-off made the streams too murky

to fish, especially Acme Creek and the river below where the creek joined it, so David and Fuller drove up to the high country. Beyond Fuller's cabin, the road steepened and narrowed to one track and four-wheel drive was required. Fuller stopped and shifted down where the Forest Service sign advised. No one else was out, and for the two of them, it was a private wander. The road had been built by the miners a hundred years ago, and as the jeep moaned slowly up the grades and switchbacks, David half expected to meet an ore wagon, brakes set, easing down to the smelter in the valley. Several times they had to stop the jeep to fill deep holes in the road so they could pass, or move a blown-down tree, or stack rocks in a swift stream to make it level enough to cross.

The rough dirt road wound through the alpine and sub-alpine zones, up through the pine and aspen, then into the fir and spruce spaced out near the timberline. Beyond the last trees was the tundra, low-profile, matted bushes adapted to survive the drying effects of the sun and wind, and beyond that, the rocky feldfields and talus slopes angling upward to the peaks themselves.

Most of the mines were in the trees just below timberline. There the trees had provided timber for the mines and logs for the cabins, and the loose dirt was eroded from the rock ledges exposing the outcroppings which marked the mineral veins.

David and Fuller stopped at the base of an ochre mine dump piled thirty feet above the road and retained by a rotting log cribwork. Rusty groundwater drained down the face of the dump in a stained russet ditch. David and Fuller got out of the jeep and made their way slowly up and around the base of the dump, stopping to heft rock fragments, breaking the heavier ones with their geologists' hammers.

"There is a fair amount of mineral still here," Fuller said, inspecting a rock he had just broken.

"I'm not surprised," said David. "The freight costs were so high they only shipped out the high-grade ore. Lots of people have actually mined these dumps since. For awhile, a couple of school teachers from Gunther worked up here somewhere in the summers, bulldozing the ore from the dumps into a dump truck and hauling it to the smelter in Salt Lake. They said they made several thousand dollars every summer."

"Isn't this the Tabasco Mine?" Fuller said, looking around. Part of

the weathered shaft house still stood at the side of the dump.

"Great name, isn't it. They had colorful names for the mines didn't they? The Ocean Wave, Red Rover, Belle of the West, Mountain Lion."

"My favorite was Big Casino."

"Big business."

"Just another industry. With its dark side. Labor strikes. Injuries. Deaths. "

"I'd rather think of mining in a more romantic sense," David said smiling. "You know, prospectors living and working in the high country, in a wholesome sort of work-therapy program."

"Nobody's that romantic."

David and Fuller made their way around the side of the yellow dump and climbed up to its flat top. Two narrow tracks ran from the edge of the dump back into the blackness of a small tunnel. Timbers boxed the tunnel entrance and a crudely lettered KEEP OUT sign was nailed to one of the posts. David looked in. Cool air met his face. Water dripped into a shallow pool just inside the darkness. He knew better than to go in. It was timbered. "Never go in the timbered mines," his father had told him. Some of the mines were in hard rock and didn't have to be timbered. They were safer. But if a mine needed timbers in 1870 to keep it from caving in, it "damn sure" needed them now. Those timbers are a hundred years older.

David looked into the mine as far as he dared. Then he and Fuller walked to the edge of the dump and sat down. Stretched out before them in a wide panorama, the gray peaks and cirques were nearly at eye level. Below them to the left, the valley that they had driven up, v-ed away stereoscopically, the superimposed valley sides sloping left and right into a weaving centerline that marked the course of the stream bed.

Mountains were in every direction. To the south they could see most of the San Juan range that covered nearly 10,000 square miles of south-western Colorado, a huge square of alpine wilderness with thirteen peaks over 14,000 feet, crossed by only one paved road. From this majestic uplift, water from rain and snowpack flowed down a radial drainage area, the headwaters of nine major rivers. Survivors of a terrible geologic storm, the San Juans were produced by a collision of such force that the surface of the earth was crumpled and creased like

aluminum foil. Then in a series of eruptions that lasted thirty million years, volcanoes covered the area, forty miles across, with four thousand feet of lava and ash. The volcanoes collapsed over and over into huge circular calderas, and between collapses, mineral rich magma seeped into the broken rocky mass, hardening into the ore-bearing veins, the mineral riches that determined the region's history. Snow from millions of winters fused into glacial ice that slowly carved the area like giant rasps, sculpting the peaks into the broken horns and long ridges, the cirques and U-shaped valleys typical of glaciation. As the glaciers began to melt, the debris-laden run-off cascaded down the tilted surface, cutting canyons and ravines through the soft volcanic crust, spilling it out into the new valleys as huge alluvial fans.

"Pretty easy to see the caldera from here," David said. "That ring of mountains there," his arm made a wide circle indicating a broken egg shell ring of jagged peaks. "It formed the edge of the volcanic caldera that collapsed in on itself after the eruptions. Maybe 30 million years ago. Erosion and the glaciers have pretty much filled in the craters, but you can still see the shape. This whole area, twenty to thirty miles across, was volcanoes. Before the area was warped up into mountains and eroded, it was covered with lava. Some of it as far away as Antelope Park. I found some shale on a mine dump there, layered right out. Apparently came from a lake bed where the ash settled out after each eruption. Must be twenty layers. There's even lava on top of Uncompahgre Peak."

"At 14,000 feet?"

"Pieces of it were left up there after the erosion and glaciers tore everything else down and left these peaks. Red Mountain there, that's the old cone." David pointed to a reddish mountain in the center of the caldera, granular and completely bare at the top like a strawberry sandpile. "It's high grade alunite ore. Aluminum. A few years ago a mining company wanted to bulldoze the mountain down and haul it off. Just like they have done at the molybdenum mine over at Climax."

"I heard about that," Fuller said.

"Fortunately, the whole area opposed it. Organized a letter writing campaign. All the summer tourists pitched in. Finally the Bureau of Land Management denied their permit."

David was looking out over the mountains. "Imagine what mining

companies would do to this country now with trucks and roads, pipelines, and leaking, toxic, tailing ponds everywhere?" he said. "See those yellow streaks on the mountains there? That's uranium. It's everywhere. You should have seen the helicopters here when the government was offering ten thousand dollars for every new uranium find."

For David, people in the mountains were a problem he had never completely resolved. Somehow, it was all right for the prospectors and the miners to have been here. It was as if they were a part of the country like the rocks themselves. It was as if history had begun with them. But the others, the ones who came later, with their helicopters and their pipes and their lights, they were interlopers, intruders, defilers in a holy place.

It was a romantic notion, and he knew it. He knew that the miners had abused the country. He had seen the pictures, the photographs of the shaft houses, the trams, the mills. But their scars had healed. The timbered slopes they had stripped to stump-bare had regrown, the smoke from their mill fires had cleared away, their trash had decomposed. The reality of their offenses was gone. Their careless, muddy tracks in the garden were overgrown.

"Have you ever been to Carson City?" David asked.

"The ghost town?"

"Yes."

"No, but I've wanted to," said Fuller.

"It's just on the other side of that peak." David was pointing to a bare, gray peak striped with erosions and slides. "Why don't we go up there on the way back," David suggested. "We have time."

"Another good idea," Fuller said. "Why don't you drive?"

"Let's go," said David. The two men made their way down off the mine dump and got into the jeep. As David drove away he glanced quickly at the sky. He had been caught in Carson once in an early snowstorm and had to spend the night. He wanted to avoid repeating that experience.

The road to Carson turned off the Acme Creek road five miles above Henson. It had been built during the mining boom of the 1880s to haul ore down from the mines at Carson and supplies back up from Henson. For the first few miles the rough track followed a stream up a narrow

rocky canyon. The road was nearly at stream level, and the spring run-off had washed away all the loose dirt and rocks leaving only a series of stone steps. At the head of the canyon the road crossed the streambed and climbed a steep shelf road just wide enough for one jeep.

"I remember meeting another jeep here once," David said to Fuller without looking away from the road. "I didn't want to back up and neither did the other driver. He pulled up on the hillside so far I thought he was going to flip over. My wheels were nearly hanging off the edge. It looked as if there would be barely enough room to pass, but as we inched closer together, I could see that the side mirrors were going to hit. The other driver and I got the idea at the same time. We each folded in our mirrors and passed with less than an inch between us. We shook hands as we passed." Fuller looked down at the streambed a hundred feet below.

The road wound up the side of the canyon wall in a series of tight hairpin turns. David picked his way carefully along the rough road, trying to keep up speed enough to prevent a stall, but moving slow enough to avoid the large rocks that might, if taken too fast, ground the jeep, or tip it over, or wrench the steering wheel from his hands. Each turn was a separate adventure. As he approached each one, David strained up to see over the hood of the jeep, picking a line though the turn that would avoid as many obstacles as possible.

On one section of the steep road, the unprotected drop-off to the streambed below was over three hundred feet. The motor of the jeep labored as it rocked along perilously close to the edge of the road. Neither man spoke. Both felt fear and, at the same time the stimulation of a danger that could just be dealt with. On one tight turn, David glanced over to see a patch of lupine, beautiful, unaware, crowding the sunny hillside.

Rounding a wooded turn, the road leveled off, passed through an aspen grove and out into a meadow. David stopped the jeep. There ahead, in the lee of an overhanging cirque, just at the tree line, was what was left of Carson City, a group of old wooden buildings, weathered the color of cinnamon. It seemed strange to see the buildings, so complete, sitting there in the empty meadow. No people. No streets. It was as if the buildings had been set down in this unlikely spot for storage and then forgotten.

David drove the jeep the last hundred yards and stopped beside the old hotel. The one-story building was roofless. Inside, the small square rooms were interconnected, one to another, without hallways. The floorboards, still intact, were burned in places where sheep-herders or hunters had built fires. The window frames were broken out.

Next to the hotel, the stable still roofed, listed to windward. The tongue-and-groove ceiling was still intact.

"Thank goodness for this roof," David said, looking around the stable. "I spent a cold night in here once."

"On purpose?" Fuller asked with mock concern.

"No," said David, "I was just up here late one summer fooling around, like we are now, and it started snowing. I couldn't believe it." Fuller made a dramatic gesture of looking out of the window at the sky. "I came in here to wait out the storm, but it didn't stop. It was snowing so hard I couldn't even see the hotel, so I couldn't leave. It snowed hard 'til dark, and by then I had made up my mind that I had to stay."

"But your folks..." Fuller said.

"Fortunately that was a summer when I had come out here alone. They would have been worried sick looking for me. I was okay. It's just that they wouldn't have known that."

"What did you do, build a fire?" Fuller asked.

"Right there," David pointed to the corner of the building. "And I can tell you two other things."

"What's that?"

"See those tongue-and-groove boards on the ceiling?"

Fuller looked up at the ceiling. "What about them?"

"Well, for one thing, I spent some time that night trying to figure why they would go to all the trouble to haul fancy milled lumber all the way up to this place for a stable ceiling."

"Why did they?"

"I don't know."

"What's the second thing?" Fuller asked.

"Those boards. There are a hundred and forty of them."

"Are you sure?"

"REAL sure," David said.

David and Fuller wandered for awhile through the seven other buildings that made up the silent little community and then came back and sat on the grass against the wall of the stable where they could look out past the buildings, across the little meadow. At the end of the valley, the humped back of Sunshine Peak filled the sky, pied with cloud shadows that lay across the slopes like limp, gray cutouts.

"You can almost hear voices, can't you," David said. Fuller nodded.

"What a place to live," David said.

"Those miners weren't so dumb."

"Hard work, but what a place. The outdoors. All this scenery. Privacy. A man could leave the East and disappear here."

"Like you have?" Fuller said. David smiled.

"Did the miners stay up here all winter?" Fuller asked.

"They did here. At least some of them. The mine tunnels were over that ridge," Fuller pointed to the large cirque which rose abruptly 600 feet behind the buildings. "The men worked over there and lived over on this side. The wind kept the snow level here blown down." David glanced into the trees to see that the tallest stumps were only a foot or two high.

"You know what the miners used to do in the winter?" David said, looking at Fuller. "In the 1880s the telephone company strung lines from Henson up here and to several of the other mining camps. For entertainment, the miners had telephone concerts."

"Telephone concerts?"

"The operator would open all the lines, so they could hear each other, like one large party line. The miners here and at Rose's Cabin, Mineral Point and Ouray took turns performing while the others listened. There were flute solos, zither solos, banjo, tenor horn. Several sang. One fellow used to yodel. Good, huh?"

"You're kidding," said Fuller.

"No," said David. "The newspapers carried accounts of these Telephone Concerts as they were called."

"How resourceful."

"It's easy to underestimate our ancestors, isn't it? Too easy to assume that because their life was simpler the people were somehow naive, less intelligent, less observant. Less playful. "

"It's a trap of arrogance."

The two men sat in the old town and talked until the sun dropped behind the peaks leaving the valley in shadows with the sky above

still bright.

"We better get going," David said. "We don't want to be driving down out of here in the dark, and one cold night up here is enough for me."

On the way back down the mountain, the jeep crept, lurching and moaning over the streambed that passed for a road. "Can you imagine building this road," Fuller said, holding on to the handle on the dashboard to keep from being bounced about. "No graders. No bulldozers. It must have been pick and shovel work."

"Almost certainly," David agreed. "But some of the old road builders were good at it. They made it a business. Like Otto Meers. He built roads to mining towns, hauled goods over them, and charged everyone else a toll. In no time he had paid for it. Next he established a newspaper in the town and praised the virtues of the town. One old broadside I saw even showed a paddle-wheel steamer in the Gunther River at Henson! Then, if he was lucky, he sold the right of way to the railroad and moved on to another project."

Although David and Fuller had known each other only a short while, they enjoyed each other's company and were finding more and more in common. They both liked the severity, the majesty, the history of the high country and respected each other's separate knowledge. Their interests potentiated each other's, filling in the blanks. They were complementary. A fortunate coincidence, David thought, as he turned onto the main road.

They drove back to town through the evening. The sky was peacock blue and just dark enough to see the stars.

"You know," said David, "it's amazing what those men attempted."

"The miners?" Fuller asked.

"Well, them too, but I was thinking about Hawthorne. I mean, can you imagine walking across these mountains in the winter? It's amazing."

Fuller nodded.

The two men rode quietly, comfortable enough with each other now to tolerate silence. Just south of town, David turned onto the road that led to his cabin. He crossed the river, drove up the hill, and stopped the jeep by the back door.

"Well," said Fuller stretching, "that was a good day."

"It was that," David agreed, getting stiffly out of the jeep. "Thanks for taking your jeep."

Fuller slid over to the driver's seat. "Thanks for the tour."

David walked to the back door and stood as Fuller put the jeep in gear and started to drive off. Fuller stopped, put his elbow out of the window and leaned toward David. "That Hawthorne trip," he said, "it was amazing, wasn't it?"

"I can't imagine it."

"You know what is most amazing about it to me?"

"What's that?"

"They almost made it."

Fuller smiled and drove off. David watched the headlights wind down the hill to the main road and then he went inside. On the wall by the door was a calendar. David tore off the top date and looked at it as he walked toward the trash basket. October 2. That's funny, he thought. That's the day Hawthorne left St. Louis.

15

Fuller reached the woman at the store in Cimarron on Monday. She said Mrs. Winchell was back home and could see them on Tuesday if that was a good day for them. They drove over, arriving just after noon to avoid being at a stranger's house at lunchtime.

The woman who met them at the door was small and very old. She wore a large squash blossom necklace over a loose purple top that was belted with a concho belt. She looked like a very pale Indian.

"Good morning," she said holding open the screen door after greeting them. Her hair was dyed for the most part a sooty black and, except for several stray wisps, was pulled back into a loose bun. "So, you are the historians," she said, inspecting them, blinking.

"Well, " David began...

"Everyone is a historian these days," she said. "Never mind. Come in. Let's go in and see what the historians want." She used a cane and walked carefully with the rhythmic lurch of hip disease. She led them from the entry alcove through an archway into a dark room with two leather couches and a worn Ganado rug. Along one wall was a stone fireplace. The opposite wall was all French doors. Heavy wooden shutters had been closed over the glass shutting out the light.

"Please sit," she said, arranging the cane across her lap. Indian blankets were draped over all the furniture, and pottery was everywhere, on every shelf, on every table. This looks like an archaeologist's house, David thought.

"And where are you gentlemen from?" she asked, looking from David to Fuller and back. Her voice was thin and reedy and quivered slightly. It was a moist, hoarse voice which sounded as if she needed to clear her throat, but she never did.

"We live in Henson, Colorado," David said. He didn't see any advantage in going into his background with her.

"And you have come all the way over here to ask me about Apache Pass." Obviously the woman at the store had prepared her.

"Yes, we are interested in Apache Pass, and the couple at the store told us that you know more about it than anyone else," David said, hoping to make a good impression.

"Adelle told me you were doing research." She accented the first syllable. "Not too many people know about Apache Pass."

"The couple at the store said that it was an old shortcut from here to the Taos Valley and the Rio Grand."

"That's right," she said. David and Fuller waited while she took something that was bothering her from the tip of her tongue. She continued. "When I was a girl my father drove cattle over Apache Pass. It was two days shorter than going around to the south." She shifted uncomfortably in the chair, then finding a better spot, leaned back slowly.

"So you're from Cimarron?" David asked.

"I was born here," she said. "Raised here. If I have my way about it, I will die here."

David didn't know what to say. He coughed and looked at Fuller.

Unexpectedly, she continued. "We had a ranch, just west of town. It was near Apache Pass. My great-grandfather came out on the Santa Fe Trail from Ohio and just stayed. There was almost no one else here then. Except Indians." David smiled to encourage her to go on. "That was 1831," she added.

David looked around the room. The clock on the mantle had stopped one day at 10:34. "This is a nice place," he said.

"Horace and I moved into this house when we were married. He had it built. He never let me look in it 'til the day we moved in. Christmas day." She paused, then turned to Fuller. "Why are you interested in Apache Pass?"

"Well," Fuller began, "it's a long story. Both of us," he gestured toward David, "have been interested in an expedition led by James Hawthorne in 1848. He was trying to cross the San Juan Mountains in the winter, but it ended in disaster and all the men died except Hawthorne and his guide."

"Bill Walker," she finished.

"Yes," said Fuller, sitting forward. He glanced quickly at David. "You know about the Hawthorne expedition?" he confirmed.

"Of course," she said. "Bill Walker could have gotten them through if Hawthorne had listened to him," she said bluntly. "Everybody knows that. You're historians. You know that."

"I think you're right," David said.

"Well," Fuller resumed carefully, "we found a copy of a letter in Santa Fe, in the museum there, that said Walker was killed on Apache Pass."

"That's right, too," she said quickly. "Hawthorne sent Bill Walker back into the mountains to rescue the baggage. Hawthorne made them leave it there. Bill Walker found it of course, and on the way back he was murdered."

"What was he doing in Apache Pass?" Fuller asked, pressing her gently. "That's not on the way back to Santa Fe."

"I don't know what he was doing there," she said. There was a defensive tone in her voice. "But that's where he was killed. My father told me that. And his father told him." She paused after each sentence as if she were finished. "Bill Walker was well-known around here, you know. He trapped all over these mountains. Quite a man, Bill Walker was. He lived with the Indians, but he never was one of them," she frowned. "Some said he had an Indian wife, but I don't believe it. He led the first wagons into Santa Fe. He came with the first traders. He showed them the way."

"So he knew this area?" Fuller said to her.

"Every inch of it," she said firmly.

"I have heard that after the Utes killed Walker, they gave him a chief's burial, " Fuller said. He leaned forward, his elbows on his knees. "Why would they do that? Why would they kill him and then give him a chief's burial ? If he lived with them, wouldn't they have recognized him?"

"Well, you see," she said, picking at something on her skirt, "I don't know anything about any chief's burial. No one ever found his body, you know. But anyway," she looked right at Fuller, blinking, "the Indians didn't kill Bill Walker. There wouldn't have been any Indians in Apache Pass in the winter. They wintered down in the valley.

At Pagosa Springs."

Fuller glanced at David. "Then who killed Walker?" Fuller asked. David leaned forward in anticipation.

"Why the Mexicans, of course," she said calmly. "Moro Mexicans." David's eyes met Fuller's briefly. "Have you ever heard of Moro?" she asked; then without waiting for their answer she went on. "It's twelve miles from here. Between here and Santa Fe. The Spanish sent their criminals there. Branded them on the cheek with a hot iron so they could be recognized at a distance. Told them that if anyone left they would be hunted down and killed." Then as if she had just remembered, "Do you know how the Spanish killed their prisoners? They tied a rope on each arm and leg and pulled them apart with horses. That's the Moro Mexicans," she said with contempt. "They stole from everyone. Even raided the wagons on the trail if the wagon trains were small enough. Disguised themselves as Indians. They're one of the reasons the wagons stopped at the Arkansas River and 'grouped up.' Out on the plains the Apaches got them. Around here it was the Moro Mexicans. They were famous for murders. Especially Anglos. All the trappers knew it. They wouldn't go anywhere near Moro. The Moro Mexicans," she said adamantly. "They're the ones that murdered Bill Walker."

David began. He wanted to know how she knew, how she was so sure, but she continued before he could ask her.

"My great-grandfather knew a Mexican man who told him all about it. The Mexicans were the ones who took the baggage. And the mules. And the money. Silver coins. He told my grandfather that the Mexicans found Bill Walker in a camp in Apache Pass and sat down with him. They wanted the mules and the money. When Bill Walker said no, they killed him and took the money. And the mules. It's been a secret in Moro ever since."

"You say your great-grandfather was told this by a man from Moro?" Fuller asked.

"He ran away from Moro and my great-grandfather hid him. He worked for my great-grandfather. The two of them made the ranch work. They became good friends, and he never forgot that my great-grandfather took him in. He told my great-grandfather why he had left Moro and told him to keep the secret. My father told me as he was dying. "

A cat walked slowly into the room, hesitated for a moment looking at David and Fuller, then effortlessly jumped into the old lady's lap. She stroked the cat absentmindedly. "Bill Walker was a very unusual man, you know. He was a wonderful man. He wandered this country for forty years, scarcely ever going near civilization. He trapped alone." The cat looked pleased. "Oh, sometimes he would go out with a group of men to trap and would stay with them for a few days. Then one morning they would wake up and he would be gone. Left in the night. Like an Indian. No one really even knew where he trapped, but he showed up everywhere. He was no place and every place. He was like a spirit. The Indians said he could fly." She smiled proudly.

"Well," Fuller started to ask another question, but she ignored him.

"My great-grandfather saw Bill Walker once," she said. "He said Walker was over six feet tall. Stringy and thin. His face was all scarred from the pox." She spoke as if she could see him. "He had a long beard and red hair that he wore like the trappers, down to his shoulders. When he rode he leaned forward on the pommel of the saddle, his rifle always crossed in front of him, and his stirrups were so short that his breeches rubbed up to his knees. He wore a buckskin shirt and a cap made out of a blanket, the top corners drawn up into dog-like ears. My great-grandfather said he looked like his Satanic Majesty himself." She thought about that for a moment. "Look," she said, pushing on the chair to get to her feet. The cat, surprised, jumped away. Mrs. Winchell steadied herself for a moment with her cane and then walked carefully across the room to a bookshelf. "These are my treasures." She spoke without looking at the men. "Thompson's book on Bill Walker. Ruxton here. He trapped with him for three days. And this," she took down a book, "Hamilton's book on the prairie. A whole chapter in here." She held the book to her chest with one hand for a moment and then put it back on the shelf. She turned to the silent men and then made her way back across the room to the mantle. "This is a sketch I did from the descriptions. This is what Bill Walker looked like. I know it." She looked fondly at the picture, then walked over and handed it to David.

It was a pencil drawing of a man's head. The metal frame was ornate. The man staring out looked tired. His face was sharp and

drawn and dotted with little scars. He looked familiar. He looks like Willie Nelson, David thought. He handed the picture reverently to Fuller.

"Bill Walker was a very superstitious man, you know, "she said, taking the picture from Fuller, and slowly sitting, still holding the picture. "He told Ruxton that he was convinced that if a bear ever touched him that he would die. He wore a single grizzly claw around his neck. To keep the bears away. He never took it off." She looked at the picture again and spoke slowly. "My great-grandfather's friend, he told my great-grandfather that the men in Moro were paid by a man to kill Walker. They were told that Walker was traveling with a lot of silver and that if they killed him they could have it. The man only wanted one thing."

David and Fuller were spellbound. "What was that?" David managed to ask.

She looked over at the men, as if she had been momentarily distracted. "The bear claw Bill Walker wore around his neck. He knew that Bill Walker would never give up the claw, and that if they had it, it would mean that Bill Walker was dead."

"That's fascinating," Fuller said. "But," he was trying to be careful, "how do you know he was telling your great-grandfather the truth?"

"He gave him this," she said, and pulled from underneath her blouse a single bear claw she was wearing around her neck on a leather thong. It was curved and black. It was at least five inches long. A grizzly claw.

"Look at this," she said without having to as she took the claw from around her neck and held it out for the two men to see. David and Fuller strained forward. She turned the claw over and was pointing to the underside. "Can you read this?" Scratched into the underside of the claw was the word SOLITAIRE.

"My god," Fuller breathed. "Old Solitaire!"

"That's what Bill Walker called himself," she continued matter-of-factly. "Old Solitaire." She smiled fondly at the claw, turning it in her hands. David and Fuller sat transfixed. The only remaining question formed immediately in David's mind and his voice broke slightly as he asked it.

"Who was the man," he said hurriedly. "The Mexicans said a man

told them to kill Walker. Who was the man?"

Ruth Winchell turned her head slightly and looked up from the claw as if slightly surprised. "Why, Hawthorne, of course."

JANUARY 12

Snow began again at daylight none of men has come down all presumed dead only W & I remain W out for two hours this AM he looks surprisingly fit I fear the unlawful worst reluctant to sleep or walk before him in these starving times tomorrow cache baggage take rifles & blankets & head to the river would that I had taken the inviting pass that was there

16

"What a story!" David said, as they sat in the car. They were too anxious to talk about what they had just heard to drive away. "I mean it's perfect, isn't it? Hawthorne stays around Blanco long enough to recover, and while he is there, he hears about Moro. Then he sends Walker back for the baggage, tells the Mexicans the story about the silver and arranges for them to go with Walker. Then Hawthorne takes off for California without waiting for the claw. A perfect alibi. If it worked, it worked. If not, he was no worse off. No one else knew about the silver. Hawthorne could be sure the Mexicans would not tell the Army the real story. And that would account for the clothes the Mexicans had. The Mexicans didn't get the clothes from the Indians." David thought for a minute, reviewing the scenario. "But," he said, turning in his seat, "the Army must have known that it was unusual for Indians to be in the mountains that time of year."

"Didn't seem to occur to them, did it?" Fuller said. "Calhoun seemed suspicious though, didn't he? At least his letters sounded that way."

David continued. "Hawthorne even wrote back asking if his things had been recovered."

"Maybe he was hoping to get some news of Walker at the same time without asking directly?" Fuller suggested.

"You know," David said with pleasant resignation, "You really had all this pretty well figured out."

"Criminal mind," Fuller said. "Speaking of criminal minds," he went on, "there's something else about this whole thing that bothers me."

"What's that?" David asked.

"Well, think about it." Fuller turned toward David. "The people of Moro murder a famous guide. Someone that everyone around here knows. The story is somehow kept secret for a 150 years, perhaps initially out of fear, perhaps later out of shame. Then after all that time, within three months, two Anglos, maybe even police or FBI, who knows, come to their town asking about their secret. "

A chill swept through David. "I didn't tell you about the man with the binoculars, did I?"

"What man?" Fuller asked.

"When I went to Moro," David said, "after I talked to that guy at the store about Hawthorne. As I drove away he was standing in the driveway with another fellow who was watching me with binoculars."

"You never told me that." Fuller seemed concerned.

"It didn't make any sense 'til now," David said. Fuller started the car and drove off thinking. They rode in silence for several miles.

"That makes it even more worrisome, doesn't it," Fuller said finally.

"Ummm," David agreed.

"And just by chance," Fuller pointed out, "these same two men, the ones asking all the questions in Moro, turn out to be both living in Henson where they are also asking about Moro and Hawthorne."

"And?"

"The *and* is a few days later; a man in Henson, whose name just happens to be Cordova, is murdered."

"Buster?" David asked.

"Buster," said Fuller.

"What are you getting at?" Now David was concerned.

"Well, at least one other family besides the Cordovas knows who murdered Walker," Fuller said.

"Ruth Winchell?" David suggested.

"Ruth Winchell and the Hawthornes."

"Hawthornes?" David said anxiously.

"They must."

"But no one would tell his children about something like that," David protested.

"Believe me," assured Fuller. "They know."

"But, Buster? What's he got to do with all this?"

"Buster was a Cordova. He was from Moro. He knew. Suppose Buster is unreliable. Suppose two guys, the two guys asking questions in Moro, just happen to show up in Henson where Buster is living? Suppose they find Buster and he tells them all about it?"

"Now you're telling me that the Hawthornes killed Buster?" David said in disbelief."

"It would shut him up," Fuller said bluntly, "and it would certainly put the other Cordovas on notice."

"That's too far-fetched," David said, trying to dismiss it.

"Did the Americans try to kill Castro?" Fuller asked rhetorically. "Did the Bulgarians, or even the Russians, try to kill the Pope? Who killed John Kennedy? And Bobby?"

"You are cynical!"

"Believe me, the Hawthornes are powerful people. If they wanted it done, it would get done."

"But murder," David said, still reluctant. "It was a hundred and fifty years ago. It couldn't be that important now."

"It couldn't?"

Could it, David wondered? What had started out as an academic exercise was taking an ugly turn. Accusing a family's ancestors of a murder over one hundred years ago was one thing, but accusing the living ones of a present day murder was quite another. He hesitated to think where this might lead. Suppose they did pursue the possibility that the

Hawthorne family had Buster murdered? What if it were not true? Or still worse, what if it were?

17

David and Fuller drove as far as Monte Vista before it got dark. They hadn't talked much for most of the way. Neither wanted to discuss the troubling notion that the Hawthorne family might somehow be involved with Buster's death, but just then they couldn't think of anything else to talk about.

David felt confused. Could what Ruth Winchell told them be true? If so, it was a brand new story. The information Fuller had discovered about the route of the expedition, the watercolors, Conejos Creek, that was interesting enough, and it was what he had thought he wanted to learn when he came to Henson. But what they had discovered about Walker and Hawthorne, that was unexpected and more than a little frightening. Fuller seemed concerned too, David thought. Maybe that's why he was so quiet. David was thinking about the Hawthornes and how, or even whether, they could go about confirming what Ruth Winchell had told them when Fuller pulled over and stopped the car. David had been so preoccupied he hadn't realized they had entered a town.

"San Juan Cafe," Fuller announced, switching off the engine. "Best food in the valley."

"Perfect timing," said David, doubly relieved.

The cafe looked promising, David thought. It was a whitewashed cement building, pueblo style, with a brown and yellow neon CAFE sign on the roof. Beside the sign were propped two Christmas stars, unlit. There was an entrance for the bar and another for the dining room and a sign painted on the wall promised that there were truckers' tables available. No trucks were in the parking lot. There were no cars, either.

David and Fuller went in the dining-room door and sat in one of the red Naugahyde booths. A chrome jukebox selector was mounted on the wall over the napkins and the salt and pepper. No one else was in the place.

"What'll it be?" said the waitress, setting a glass of ice water in front of each of them. The plastic tag said that her name was Erlene.

"The number four Mexican dinner," said Fuller, closing the menu. "And a coke," he added.

"Chicken-fried steak and a coke for me," said David.

Fuller grinned behind his hand as the waitress walked away, writing.

"So it is true," Fuller said.

"What's that?" David asked.

"Well," Fuller explained," I read once that no real Texan could ever think of taking a trip of over 200 miles without stopping at least once for chicken-fried steak."

David smiled. "One of the four basic food groups," he said.

"And the other three?"

"Enchiladas, barbecue, and peach cobbler," David said proudly. "The best food is brown."

They talked, but neither one mentioned Ruth Winchell, or the Hawthornes. Erlene brought the cokes and two glasses. She poured the ice water in the new glasses and the two cokes in the glasses that had held the ice water. She looked at the table briefly to satisfy herself that the men were taken care of and walked away.

"I knew this was going to be a good place when we came in," said David.

"How's that?" asked Fuller, challenging him.

"Well, first of all," said David, "there is a Tabasco bottle full of toothpicks on the counter by the cash register. The flat ones. Not the round ones."

"And?"

"And the menu. "

"What about it?"

"Black back, clear plastic slips. Menu typed by hand using carbon paper. That's always a good sign. No frozen portions here."

"What else?" Fuller was playing.

"The waitress didn't introduce herself."

"Okay," Fuller consented.

"And," David continued, "she had a great waitress name."

"Erlene."

"The only better ones are Helen and Juanita. Names are important. In cafes, just like baseball."

"What's baseball got to do with it?" Fuller asked.

"I've got a friend," David confided playfully, "who says that if you tell him a guy's name, he can tell you whether or not he will make it in the major leagues."

Fuller smiled with mock exasperation.

"Eight to five Erlene won't say the "E" word," David said.

"The "E" word?"

"She won't say 'Enjoy' when she brings our order."

Erlene appeared with the plates and slid them down expertly in front of the two men. "Be anything else?" she said.

"I'm fine," said David.

"Me, too," said Fuller. Erlene walked away. The two men smiled.

"And then," said David picking up his fork, " there's the *piece de resistance*."

"I give up," Fuller smiled.

"The order book."

"Go on," Fuller said indulging him.

"Green tablet. Lined. Folds over. No carbons. Mandatory."

"You're into cafes, aren't you?" said Fuller. David gave him a you-got-it gesture with his fork and began to eat.

"How would you rate your chicken-fried steak?" Fuller asked.

"I'd say about an eight," David said through a mouthful of

chicken-fried steak. "Would have been better if the batter was brown and there was more pepper in the cream gravy. Otherwise, pretty good, I'd say."

"I'll bet you ten bucks," David said as they ate, "that there's a picture of the local high school football team behind the counter."

"I wouldn't challenge an expert."

When Erlene came to ask about desert, David told her that he wanted peach cobbler but settled for chocolate icebox pie. Fuller had blueberry. Erlene poured coffee from the pot she had brought with her.

"You know," David said with a sigh, "there are few things pie can't fix."

As the two men talked, a cowboy came in noisily, his arm around a pretty young woman with large eyes. They sat at a table near David and Fuller. Erlene met them at the table with glasses of ice water.

"I'll have a margarita with a scoop of chocolate ice cream," the cowboy said loudly. Erlene didn't flinch. "Oh, Duyane!" the girl said with mock shame.

"Look," the cowboy insisted, "it's my two favorite things and I wanta' have them together." Then turning to Erlene, "Bring some for her, too." He leaned over the girl attentively. "You'll love it."

"Fifth basic food group," Fuller said across the table to David. David winked.

"You said that you have been coming to Henson for a long time," Fuller said as they drank coffee.

"Since I was a kid. I was probably five when I first came. During the war, or perhaps just after the war."

"Probably couldn't have gotten the gasoline during the war."

"My father loved fly fishing. We always came with three other families. The men fished every day. The kids played in the water. Built dams. Pretended we were cowboys, and miners. What a great time. It was always in July. My father thought the fishing was best then. We couldn't come earlier. The water was too high. We couldn't come in September because of school. One couple always came back in September. They didn't have any children. My father was always a little jealous of them I think."

"That's quite a trip to make every year."

"I remember those trips like yesterday. The drive from Ft. Worth to Amarillo was the worst part. It was always hot. We had one of those bullet-shaped car coolers that you filled with water and clamped in the front window. Remember those?"

"I had forgotten about those."

"I remember how hot it was in the car. The car windows were small, and the back ones didn't roll down all the way. And that awful fuzzy brown upholstery."

Fuller smiled, remembering.

"On the way we stayed in motels and left early in the mornin', while it was still dark and cool. My parents put me and my brother in the back seat with pillows and told us to go back to sleep. I can still hear those big diesel trucks droning by in the darkness. We ate crackers all the way. For me the smell of vacation is still crackers in the car."

"Or ripe fruit."

"It took us three days to drive from Ft.Worth to Henson," David went on. "The first hopeful sign was when we finally got to New Mexico. Those wonderful buttes and mesas. Capulin Mountain. Raton Pass. Rabbit Ears Peak. My father always pointed out Rabbit Ears Peak. He said it was on the Santa Fe Trail. I always thought we were following the Santa Fe Trail and only learned later that we were crossing it. I wondered how he knew all that stuff. He was a doctor, too. Very busy. And I never saw him reading. Funny how you never really know your parents. After all that time."

"We stayed the second night in Trinidad. At Cawthorne's Trinidad Courts. By then we knew we were in the mountains. We could see them. The Sangre de Cristos to the west. The night air was cool for the first time and smelled of coal smoke.

We slept under blankets. In the summer!"

"The next morning we always drove to Walsenburg for breakfast. At the Alpine Rose Cafe, I always got pancakes. They must have been ten inches across. I can taste them now. Once when we were eating there – funny how you remember things – the waitress brought Kraft grape jelly in those little plastic packets. We had never seen those before. My father told the waitress that he didn't like his jelly in plastic. He wanted it spooned on the plate. My brother and I were mortified." Both men laughed, remembering how easily, and how often, they had been mortified.

Erlene appeared beside them. "You fellows all right," she said filling their coffee cups.

"Just resting," Fuller said to her.

"You're all right, then," she said, turning to go.

"Have you ever noticed," David pointed out, "how the second cup of coffee is always better than the first?"

"As a matter of fact I have," said Fuller.

"It's the cup," David said. "It's already hot. The hot cup makes it better. My mother-in-law told me that."

Fuller pursed his lips, feigning amazement.

"You know," David said, pretending not to notice Fuller's skepticism, "when I was a kid I thought the Antonio valley was awful."

"Awful?" said Fuller.

"After driving for two days and finally getting to the mountains, seeing that flat valley was always such a disappointment. And the seventy mile trip across that valley seemed to take forever. Blanca Peak just sat there out the window. It never moved. I would take a nap and wake-up, and there it would be mocking me. I never thought in those days that I would be coming back to the valley to well, work. I can call it work, can't I?"

"Research is work," Fuller said. "Writing is work. But it's fun."

"Well anyway, it was a long trip across that valley. But then suddenly, we could see cottonwood trees along the river, and

there were mountains ahead through the windshield. At noon we stopped at Alamosa, at the Safeway, for ice and groceries that would have spoiled in the heat. There were peaches. Mother bought cherries. When we got to South Pass, I knew we were there. The road branched to the north, and there was the first road sign to prove that, after three days, we really were still on the right track. HENSON 72 MILES. Only four more hours."

David sat for a minute, remembering, twirling his fork.

"They were great trips," he said. "Cafes and truck stops. Cokes in small green bottles. Curios shops. Kachina dolls and little cedar boxes. And postcards. You know," David confessed, "it seems silly now, but I never remember seeing postcards except on those trips."

The cowboy, his hat still on, and his girlfriend had finished their chocolate margaritas. "Now you've got to admit," the cowboy said to the girl," that was pretty good." David couldn't hear what the girl said, but the cowboy must have been pleased. He gave the girl a quick kiss. She saw David watching and blushed.

"Come on, hon'," the cowboy said helping her with her chair. They walked to the cash register, his hand on the small of her back. The girl went outside while the cowboy paid. Then he walked back over to the table and left a tip.

"You ought to try one of them," the cowboy said to David.

"What do you call it?" David asked.

"Sweet Jesus," the cowboy said with a grin. Then he turned and left.

"How long did your family come out here?" Fuller asked politely. He could see that David was enjoying the telling and remembering.

"We came every year 'til I was in college. After that I just got busy and quit coming. But I missed it. Ten years ago my brother and I decided to come out for a reunion, and that started it all up again. One summer Susan and I even drove out from New Hampshire with the kids. I wanted them to see the West. Then I brought my oldest boy out to college in Alamosa. Since

then I have been coming out every year."

Fuller didn't ask about Susan. Perhaps he sensed he shouldn't, and David was glad.

They finished their coffee, tipped Erlene and agreed to split the check. Erlene came to the register to take the money.

"Everything okay?" she asked, wiping her hands on her apron.

"You bet," said Fuller.

She rang up the money and handed them their change. "You all come back," she said. David pointed out the football team picture and winked at Fuller. He took a toothpick from the Tabasco bottle.

"I know it's corny," said David as they walked out, "but it makes me feel good when they say, 'you all come back.'"

"I know. It's nice, isn't it," said Fuller. "I remember, driving back here from the East a few years ago. I knew I was home when the self-service gas stations didn't make you pay before you pumped the gas."

"And the waitress didn't ask you how you wanted your hamburger cooked," David added.

Outside the night air was cool and smelled of coal smoke. The black sky was shot full of lighted holes. In the south, Orion hung like a marionette, as if suspended from the horns of the new moon. The little town was quiet except for a diesel truck that purred through the gear changes on the highway.

"You're going to write about this, aren't you?" David said to Fuller as they drove.

"Not exactly."

"What do you mean by that?"

"I mean *we* are going to write about it."

David was excited and flattered. "Hey, this is your story, Fuller. You are the one who stumbled onto the watercolors. It was your idea about Walker stealing the baggage and about Hawthorne having him killed by the Mexicans."

"And all the time you spent at the archives, digging up those letters?" Fuller countered. "Does that count? And your

idea to check on the newspapers?"

"There weren't any newspapers," David said.

"But we found Apache Pass, didn't we, and Ruth Winchell?"

"Yes, but..."

"No *Yes, but,*" Fuller insisted. "We will write it." David couldn't have hoped for this.

"But if we wrote that Hawthorne had Walker killed, the family would sue us for everything we're worth."

"Which is?"

"Well, you've got a point there," David agreed. "Still, we better check with a lawyer. What can they do to you for defamation of character?" David wondered aloud.

"Beats me," said Fuller. "But look what they did to Buster."

"You don't think they really killed Buster, do you?"

"Worrisome though, isn't it?" David certainly agreed with that.

"Maybe we could make it a novel," David suggested. "You know, add that disclaimer that any resemblance to persons living or dead is purely coincidental."

"Maybe," Fuller said.

"Do you think an academic journal would accept it?"

"Might. If the sources are good enough. Mrs. Winchell's story might be a problem."

"You might call that a personal communication," David suggested. "What do you think would happen to her?"

"That's a problem, isn't it." Fuller agreed.

They rode in silence for a while. Then David said, "What about those people in Moro? I mean, if the Hawthornes had Buster killed...?"

"They couldn't kill them all."

"Are you afraid?" David asked.

"A little," Fuller said, without looking from the road.

"Wouldn't be much of a life, hiding from the Hawthornes, would it?"

"They found Buster in Henson," Fuller said flatly, "and there aren't many better places to hide than that."

"Maybe Buster didn't have anything to do with it," David said hopefully. Neither of them believed that.

"Well, we just have to talk to a lawyer. Protect ourselves the best we can, and then see what our options are. This is too good to just let go."

David and Fuller rode, thinking.

"You know what?" David said.

"What?"

"It would make a great novel, wouldn't it?"

18

David was up at dawn drinking coffee. He had been restless all night and had finally given up sleeping when the sky lightened. It would be another hour before the sun came over the mountain and warmed the air in the valley. Through the kitchen window he could see that there was a heavy frost on the windshield of his car.

He sat looking at the map he had marked with the colored lines and X's. What a great illustration that map would make, he thought. The routes were so important to the development of the story, it would be good to use a coded illustration like that. He visualized the article, page after page, how it would begin, how it would end. He wondered if the journal would want the footnotes at the end or the bottom of each page. He liked those at the bottom best, the parenthetical notes, the accompanying comments at the bottom of the page. Articles read so much better if you didn't have to keep turning to the back. After awhile you just gave up, but so much was missed. Most of the books and articles he had read on Walker and Hawthorne were older. What was the fashion now? Fuller would know, he thought.

David had been interested in writing as long as he could remember. He loved words. In high school he had kept a journal and began trying to put his observations down on paper, partly because it was such a private satisfaction and partly, he had to admit, he wanted to impress his friends. He remembered feeling cheated, once or twice, after reading *Portrait of the*

Artist as a Young Man or *Absalom, Absalom*, that he had never been troubled by a dark inner crisis, the "sturm und drang" of adolescence, he later learned it was called. He felt deprived and would lie alone sometimes in his bed with the blinds closed and smoke, trying to feel appropriately troubled. Occasionally he was caught at it by one of his friends who had come by to see if he wanted to go to the drive-in or to the swimming pool. They thought he was very serious, moody, and he enjoyed that, believing that they, having been troubled, could see in an instant that he was and that this common unspoken bond made them closer. He was never sure that they had been troubled, but he was jealous that they might have been.

In college the one liberal arts course David had been able to squeeze into his pre-medical curriculum was a creative writing course. He wrote short stories on an old portable Remington, entered the short story contest and won second place. But he always wanted to write about something romantic, something exotic. *Write about what you know* his teacher had told them, but David didn't know about anything, at least anything that seemed worth writing about. He had not had any experiences. He had not had any pain. He was not troubled.

Reading something that he thought was well-written only made him angry. I could have written that, he thought, and he was provoked that another idea or an image had been used up before he had a chance. He was frustrated that he had so little time. Still he practiced and waited.

To his closest friends he would admit that he wanted to write a book. The thought of it excited him. The sound of the word *manuscript* was an elixir. He could feel, in his imagination, the heft of the stacked pages. He idolized writers and found that his writing mimicked the one he had most recently read. He envied what seemed to him the satisfaction they must have known, creating, putting the words in the perfect order. He enjoyed the thought of other people being stirred by the way he arranged words.

He began to suspect his motives. Writing is a selfish indulgence he thought. It's just playing in the imagination while being arrogant enough to think someone else might be interested. He began to think that it wasn't the writing at all that he liked, but the attention he might get, the envy that he would create. He was ashamed, and that was the stopper. The idea that he had nothing to say, and that even if he did, it was for all the wrong reasons. And for a time, he lost interest.

Then, after graduating from medical school, he realized that it was important for him to have a bibliography so he wrote again, and it came easy. But no novels or short stories. Instead of short stories, there were case reports. Instead of novels, medical review articles. But he was in print, and thirty articles later he had learned something. Research was fun.

He traded his Remington for a word processor. He abandoned index cards and made electronic folders. He wrote and re-wrote, not on yellow tablets but on his new magic slate. He spent two years editing a series of Civil War letters someone had given him and saw them published. Hardly a novel, but he was ready. He had the skills. He had the tools. All he needed was a project. Enter James Hawthorne. Here was a project.

David was immediately fascinated by the Hawthorne Expedition, and he was excited by the apparent lack of historical attention that it had attracted. He loved the library work, sending away for obscure books, poring over maps, poking around in the archives. He had good instincts. He was thrilled when he found new information, discovered historians' careless errors, found clues that were overlooked or misinterpreted. He began to realize that he knew more about James Hawthorne's mountain adventure than almost anyone else. What's more, he knew the country. Here finally, was something he knew. This was his story, and when he saw that a man named Walton had been killed on the expedition he knew that he would write about it.

It had been three weeks since he and Fuller had talked to

Ruth Winchell, and he worried for awhile about her. Maybe he should wait until she died. I wonder if Fuller has thought of that? At eighty-seven she can't live much longer. Maybe he should hold back. Maybe it would take that long to write it anyway. How long does it take to write a history article? How long would it be?

He poured another cup of coffee and went outside. He sat in a chair and leaned back against the cabin wall watching the morning shadows melt and run down off the mountains into the valley. On the far side of the valley, Crystal Peak was already fully lit. He could hear the river and the smell of alders was strong in the cool air. One by one the birds awoke and began to practice.

It all seemed to be happening too fast, David thought. For years he had visualized working leisurely on his project. Wallowing around in it. He had looked forward to it and had planned his retirement around it. Writing each day. Taking trips to libraries. Doing field research. Slowly assembling the puzzle that would fill his retirement with interest and purpose. He and the project would play out at about the same time. He had never yet thought about time beyond that.

Since he had returned from talking with Ruth Winchell, David had written every day. It was compelling. He made notes on scraps of paper. He kept a tablet in the car and next to the bed. Even in the bathroom. Finally he bought a tape recorder so he could make notes even while he was driving, later playing back the tapes, translating them to print.

He knew Fuller was doing the same. They still met to talk and compare notes. They ate together at the Pine Cone, and they fished until the season closed, but more and more of the time they spent working alone.

They had decided to write separately, each one completing the paper, and then they would begin to work together, using the best parts and ideas, rearranging, culling out what they did not like, re-writing.

It was such a pleasure working uninterrupted except for his

own clock. His medical practice hadn't left him much time for that. He had worked some on the Project, as he called it, mostly on winter weekends. Nights after work, he was usually too tired, or there wasn't enough time to get any momentum. A few times he had gotten caught up reading, or running down a lead and had worked late, but he quickly learned he could not get by with that .

During those years he had completed a lot of the background work. He read everything on Hawthorne and Walker that he could find and had catalogued his notes on the word processor. Even though his local library was small, the librarian had become interested in his project and had been very helpful getting books for him on inter-library loans. He made trips to Washington to the National Archives on three different occasions. He went to the Denver Public Library to see some reference material that could not be loaned. The trip he made to the Huntington Library had been the highlight. Seeing the original Kirk diaries, touching them, he felt he had been let in on a secret few others knew, taken into the confidence of the men themselves, and it had been thrilling. Meeting Fuller had brought it all together.

The phone rang. Probably Fuller, David thought, wanting to go to the Pine Cone for enchiladas.

"Hello," David said.

"Mr. Walton?" The voice wasn't Fuller's.

"Yes."

"My name is Dan Winchell. Ruth Winchell is my mother." David was puzzled. What could Winchell want with him, and how did he find him?

"I understand from Mother that you are doing research on Bill Walker and the Hawthorne Expedition?"

"Yes, I am." Maybe he has some more information, David thought.

"Mother told me you were over to talk with her. I got your number from Adelle at the store."

"Yes," David said. "She was the one who told us about your

mother and arranged for us to meet."

"Well," said Winchell, "I'm driving down this weekend to see Mother, and I'd like to stop by Henson and talk with you, if I may. I have some information that might interest you."

"Well, yes," said David. "I would like that. I would like that very much. That's very kind of you. What would be a good time for you?"

"It will take me about six hours to drive down from Denver to Henson," Winchell said. "How about two o'clock?"

"Sounds good. Let me tell you how to find me." David gave Winchell directions to his house, thanked him again and immediately called Fuller.

"Guess what?"

"You sent the manuscript in without waiting for me," Fuller joked.

"No," laughed David, "but it's not a bad idea. Guess who just called me?"

"Who?"

"Dan Winchell," David said.

"That wouldn't be a relative of our Ruth Winchell, would it?"

"Son."

"Well, I can hardly wait. What did he say?"

"He said that he had some information that he thought would interest me, and that he was driving over from Denver Saturday to see his mother and he wondered if he could stop off here and talk."

"Did he say what he had in mind?" Fuller asked.

"No, just that I would be interested."

"I don't like the sound of this. It can't be good news. Good news is on the phone. Bad news is in person."

"You are cynical," said David, but now he was thinking, too. "Maybe he wants to tell us not to publish anything 'til she dies," he suggested. "I'll bet it's that. He wants us to wait."

"My mother was ninety-four when she died," Fuller said.

"Well, I wouldn't want to wish her ill, but I don't want to wait that long. At the rate I'm going, I'll be finished in a month. How are you coming?"

"Pretty fast now. I'd say a month would be plenty." Then he added, "What time did you say he was coming?"

"Two o'clock Saturday," David said. "I gave him directions to the house. We can meet him here."

"Seems like a lot of trouble to go to for a stranger, Henson must be two hours out of his way."

"Who knows? Maybe he's got more information on Walker and the Cordovas. Maybe we'll get lucky."

"If it weren't for bad luck, I wouldn't have any luck at all," said Fuller.

Saturday was three days away.

Dan Winchell drove up to David's cabin at exactly two o'clock.

"Well, gentlemen," Winchell said, leaning forward in the chair, his elbows on his knees, his hands clasped together, "Mother said she enjoyed talking with you. She doesn't have much company you know."

"She's a remarkable lady," David said. "We had a good talk. She was very helpful."

Winchell sat smiling benevolently over his folded hands. "What exactly did she tell you?" he said.

David glanced at Fuller. He had arrived at David's cabin an hour before Winchell. He was still worried.

"Well," David said, trying to be pleasant, "she knows a lot about Bill Walker."

"That she does," Winchell said, still smiling.

"Well," David continued uneasily, "we are doing some research on James Hawthorne's expedition into the San Juans. We were interested in locating Apache Pass. We had heard that Walker was killed there. Your mother said that she was convinced of it. She told us that her father had told her about it. Apparently his father had told him."

David looked quickly at Fuller, then back to Winchell who still smiled expectantly. David continued. "She told us that she didn't believe the Ute Indians killed Walker, like everybody thinks. She said she thought Walker was killed by some Mexicans. She said her father told her that the Mexicans killed Walker."

That seemed like enough for a start, David thought. He sat back watching Winchell's reaction.

"Yes," Winchell said comfortably. "I have heard that story, too." Then he said, "She must have told you all about Bill Walker?"

"Yes," David said. "She seems to think a lot of him."

"Did she show you her picture of him?" Winchell asked.

"Yes, she did," David said kindly.

"And the bear claw?" Winchell asked.

David was surprised. "She did, actually."

Winchell sat back in his chair. He took off his glasses and put one earpiece in his mouth, thinking. "My mother," he began slowly, putting on his glasses, "is, well, Mother is a little bit eccentric," he tried out the word, "as you may have noticed. This Bill Walker thing. I'm afraid she may have misled you a bit." David looked at Fuller. Fuller's face had a resigned, "I knew it" expression.

"Misled us?" David said. "In what way?"

"Well, you see, her husband, my father, was killed shortly after I was born. He was robbed and murdered. She was devastated by this, and she has never, even after all these years, really gotten over it. She has never been quite the same. She has lived alone and for years would not even have any company. She used to ride out alone, every day, into the mountains where Dad was killed. She was convinced he was killed by some Mexicans. From Moro. It was all thoroughly investigated, but no one ever knew who did it."

Fuller was right, David thought.

Winchell continued. "Somehow," he said with a shrug, "she got interested in Bill Walker and it became, well, an obsession." He looked at David and Fuller to make sure they understood. "She read everything written about him. She even drew the sketch of him. I'm sure you saw it. She keeps it on the mantle," he said uncomfortably. "A few years ago, I found some letters. They were addressed to her and signed 'Bill Walker.' "Winchell paused. "They were in her handwriting."

David and Fuller stared at Winchell.

Winchell took a deep breath and let it out slowly. "I took her to the doctor, of course. He said that things like that were not all that unusual in older people. A sort of post stress disorder. He did not think she was in any danger. That it was safe for her to live alone, provided she could care for herself. So far she has done okay. Adelle helps her some." He sighed again. "I'm sorry," he said. "You understand."

They did.

"So, gentlemen," Winchell said slowly, "I'm afraid Mother is not a very reliable resource, shall we say?"

"But the bear claw?" David asked, hoping.

"She had me buy it for her. It seemed harmless enough. She must have scratched the name on it herself."

"And the Mexican friend of her great-grandfather's?"

"Made up," Winchell said. "Or imagined."

David and Fuller sat transfixed. Then Winchell, as if he had been through all this before, put his hands on his knees and prepared to stand. "I hope I haven't ruined it all for you," he said apologetically, "but I thought it only fair, before things got too far along. When I heard you were historians, well, I thought I should say something. I would have come sooner, but I only just heard about your visit."

"I guess better now than later," said Fuller speaking for the first time.

"Well," Winchell said, "if you gentlemen will excuse me, I've got a long trip to make." He glanced at his watch.

"Thank you for coming," David said. "It must not have been very easy for you. I appreciate it." Winchell seemed grateful. The men shook hands.

David showed Winchell to the door and thanked him again for going to the trouble. Fuller followed them out onto the porch, and they stood watching him drive away. It was David who

spoke first.

"Well," David said exasperated, "that's just ducky!"

19

Gunther is sixty miles due north of Henson. The road follows the river down out of the mountains almost all the way. For the first several miles, the road and the river run side by side, descending through a narrow canyon cut through the volcanic tuffs and breccias. At The Portal, an abrupt rocky gateway, the river canyon opens into a series of broad sage-covered benches and valleys sloping gently toward the main river.

As David and Fuller drove toward Gunther the panorama of the Elk Mountains spread out ahead of them just above the dashboard. The September clouds were so varied and so numerous that there was barely room for them in the crowded sky. Highest, and so close to the blue, and so still they might have been painted on, the wispy cirrus were motionless, as thin as smoke, broad, hasty brush strokes and vast white smudges larger than Russia. Below the cirrus, piles of scalloped, flat-bottomed cumulus floated by like lavender suds. Near the ground, ragged gray squall lines moved with the wind.

Neither David nor Fuller talked much. The news from Winchell had depressed them both and drained the enthusiasm that the discoveries of the past few weeks had generated.

At Sapinero Junction, both the river and the highway lose their identity, the west branch of the Gunther flowing into the main river and the highway merging with U.S. 65. Fuller turned the jeep east and headed to Gunther.

Gunther is a ranch town, laid out geometrically along the river. One wide main street, half a mile long, runs east and west through the town. To the north, rising for a few blocks up the foothills of the Elk Mountains, are shaded neighborhoods of brick and stucco houses with square pillared porches and small neat lawns.

The attorney's office was on the main street between the Driscol Hotel and the Early Bird Donut Shop. Fuller made a U-turn and parked at the curb.

"Well," said Fuller. "Let's see what happens."

All day Sunday, after Winchell's visit, David and Fuller had talked about what Winchell had told them. Reluctant to admit what the news from this unwelcome messenger might mean to their work, they had gone over and over what they had learned from Winchell and his mother. By Monday they had agreed that it would be good to at least talk with an attorney, and Fuller had called to arrange for the appointment.

Fuller had met Murphy Brewster when he was still teaching at the college. Brewster had helped Fuller with his legal affairs after "the accident." Maybe he could help again.

"Jack Fuller!" Brewster said, walking around the desk. "Good to see you, ol' buddy. I thought you had fallen off the edge of the earth."

Brewster was a large, pleasant man. He wore western pants, a string tie, and a white western shirt with pearl snaps.

"Nearly," Fuller said. "This is my friend David Walton." Brewster pumped David's hand.

"Sit down, sit down," Brewster insisted, pulling up chairs. "You're looking good, for an old fella'. What's been going on?"

"Oh, I bought a place up in Henson," Fuller said. "I've just been jobbin' around."

"How's Mary? "Brewster said. Brewster had worked closely with Fuller's sister during Fuller's rehabilitation.

"She's fine," Fuller said. "Still living in Delta."

"Boy, what a surprise," Brewster said, smiling warmly. "When Debbie said you had called for an appointment, I was really surprised. Has it really been three years?"

"Two short ones and one long one," Fuller said.

"Well," Brewster said, "what would a guy like you need a lawyer for?" He winked at David.

"Tell me about defamation of character liability?" Fuller asked.

"Hey, that's a big one! What do you mean?" Brewster was thinking

about the incident three years ago with the college and about Fuller's dismissal.

"Well," Fuller began, "suppose I wrote a book and in it I implied, or suggested," he was choosing his words carefully, "that a well-known man, a historical figure, had done something, let's say illegal, or even immoral?"

"Like what?" Brewster asked with a suspicious squint.

"Like murder," Fuller said.

Brewster looked over his half glasses at Fuller. "Murder?"

"Well, not exactly. Suppose he arranged for someone to be murdered?"

"You mean conspiracy," Brewster said, checking, seeking precision.

"I suppose so."

Brewster took a breath and leaned back in his chair. "That's a serious accusation, my friend," he said, frowning.

"I know," said Fuller.

"What are we talking about here, exactly," Brewster asked.

"It's a long story."

"I've got nothing else scheduled," Brewster said, taking a yellow pad from a drawer and putting it ceremoniously on his desk. He picked up a pen and looked up at Fuller, waiting.

"Well," Fuller began again, "James Hawthorne..."

"*The* James Hawthorne?" Brewster verified, pen poised.

"The James Hawthorne," Fuller confirmed.

Brewster's eyebrows acknowledged as he wrote. "Go on," he said.

"James Hawthorne led an expedition from St. Louis in the winter of 1848 headed for California, scouting a central route through the Rockies for the railroad." Brewster nodded as he wrote. "They got lost in the mountains near Monte Vista and everyone but Hawthorne and his guide died. Probably froze. Or starved. There has been a lot of speculation about just who was to blame for the disaster. Hawthorne, of course, blamed the guide. He said the guide didn't know where he was going. But the guide was very experienced. He had trapped all over the San Juans."

"Bill Walker, wasn't it?" Brewster asked without looking up.

"Right. Anyway, afterwards, Walker went back into the mountains to rescue the baggage and was killed, supposedly by the Indians.

The Utes."

"And you have evidence of this?" Brewster asked.

"Some correspondence from the army and some from a James Calhoun, who was the Indian Agent in Santa Fe at the time. But, it gets better."

"Go on," Brewster said.

"Some Mexicans were found with some of the dead man's clothes. Saddles and things, but they told the army that they had gotten the things from the Indians."

Brewster looked up, confused. "Indians or Mexicans?"

"Well," Fuller continued, "the historians who have written about this expedition have all used the army reports. According to these reports, the Mexicans said that the Indians killed the guide in revenge."

"Revenge?" Brewster asked.

"Apparently the summer before, the guide had been a scout for an army party that made some raids on Ute camps over near Pueblo. I'm not sure if that was true." Fuller waited while Brewster finished writing. "Anyway," Fuller continued, "Hawthorne was in the process of running for president at the time, and I think this whole expedition was staged for that. It occurred to me that it would not have gone well for Hawthorne if it got out that he was to blame for the deaths of thirty-one men."

"And you think Walker would have said that?" Brewster asked.

"He might have," Fuller said. "It was mentioned in the campaign the next year."

"And Walker would have been available to comment, presumably?" Brewster said.

"Exactly."

"Well," Brewster said, "Hawthorne was leader of the expedition."

"Yes," agreed Fuller, "and to that extent he was responsible, but he made it look as if he was a victim, misled by an incompetent guide. He was a hero, of sorts, for surviving the ordeal."

Brewster nodded. "And you think that Hawthorne had the Indians kill Walker?" Brewster said, looking at Fuller.

"Or the Mexicans," Fuller said.

"Well," Brewster said thoughtfully, "I would think about that

for awhile, if I were you. This is all pretty circumstantial. It strikes me that you don't have enough of a case to call the man a murderer."

"David did go to the National Archives to check on army records there, but there wasn't much else available. Just one letter reporting the death of Walker. Nothing in Santa Fe either. Wouldn't you think that the failure of an expedition like Hawthorne's would have attracted some official attention? And the death of his guide? Especially if he was killed by the Indians. There are all sorts of army documents and reports dealing with battles with the Indians, or trouble that the Indians were causing. But nothing else about the Indians, or Mexicans, murdering Hawthorne's guide."

Brewster was interested.

"What's more," said Fuller, "all of the 1849 issues of the Santa Fe newspaper are missing from the museum and from the archives. That's the only year missing." Brewster seemed about to interrupt him. "There's more," Fuller said. "Three weeks ago, David and I met an old woman in Cimarron. We were looking over the country where the Indians were supposed to have killed Walker. She's eldery. She was raised in Cimarron. She told us that not only was Walker killed by Mexicans and not the Indians but also that it was Hawthorne who put them up to it."

Brewster stopped writing and looked up at Fuller. "How would she know that?"

"Her father told her. And his father had told him. Apparently this man, her great-grandfather, had a hired hand, a Mexican man from Moro who assured him it was true."

"That's hearsay," Brewster said, frowning.

"I know," said Fuller," but suppose it's true?"

"Suppose it isn't?" challenged Brewster. "It might be one thing to discuss that from an academic point of view, I mean as a theory or hypothesis." He waved his hand to dismiss those considerations. "But if you're planning on publishing circumstantial evidence and using it to accuse a man of conspiracy to murder, well, I'd think about that one for awhile if I were you. The Hawthorne family would be all over you like a nineteen-dollar paint job. Relatives would come out of the woodwork for a piece of you, ol' buddy."

He added, "I don't think a publisher would touch it."

"I thought that's what you would say," Fuller said.

"That's asking for it," said Brewster.

"How does Oliver Stone get by with suggesting that the CIA killed Kennedy?" Fuller challenged.

"Well," Brewster said, "the CIA is an organization. It doesn't have individual rights. No liability there."

"What about the director," Fuller asked. "Wouldn't Stone's accusation impugn the character of the CIA director?"

"That's an entirely different matter."

"Well," Fuller said, it gets even more complicated. Wednesday David got a call from the woman's son..."

"What's her name, by the way," Brewster interrupted.

"Winchell. Ruth Winchell." Brewster wrote it down. "Well," Fuller went on, "her son called to say that he had heard that we were talking to his mother about Walker and the expedition. He said he had something to tell us that he thought we would be interested in."

"His name?"

"Dan Winchell. He said that he was on the way from Denver down to his mother's and that he would stop by and talk to us."

"On his way to Cimarron? Isn't that a little out of the way?"

"He said he didn't mind."

"OK," said Brewster," what did he tell you?"

"He said that his mother had made the whole thing up. Imagined it." Brewster had stopped writing. "He told us that his mother had this 'thing,' as he put it, about Walker. That she was obsessed by him. That she was convinced that she," Fuller paused, "that she had communicated with him."

"With Walker, you mean?" Brewster asked skeptically.

"Yes," Fuller admitted. "We did see some things. She had a bookcase full of books about Walker and she had drawn this picture. It was a sketch of what she said Walker looked like. Framed it."

"Well..., "Brewster started to protest.

"That's not all." Fuller glanced quickly at David whose expression said, "May as well." "Winchell told us that his mother had letters addressed to her and signed 'Bill Walker.' He said they were in her

own handwriting."

Brewster rolled his eyes at the ceiling and put down his pen. "Wait a minute. Wait a minute," he said, taking off his glasses with a frustrated swipe. "This lady's a first class kook! I mean, she's crazy as an outhouse rat! Not only," he said, getting up and walking around the desk, "is her story, even IF it were true, totally circumstantial hearsay, but now you're telling me that there is more than an even chance that she has made the whole thing up. And what's more, believes it herself? You don't need a lawyer. You need a shrink!" Brewster had leaned up against the front of the desk and had his arms folded across his chest.

"Unless he's lying."

Brewster looked at the ceiling, patting his pursed lips. "To protect his mother," he said, still looking at the ceiling.

"Exactly," said Fuller. David looked quickly at Fuller. They had never discussed that.

"So," Brewster summarized, walking around the room as if addressing a jury, "Winchell learns that his eccentric mother is accusing a prominent family's most famous relative of conspiracy to murder and that she has blabbed about it to a couple of historians who plan to quote her in print. He can't very well just go talk them out of it, can he? So he does something even better. He discredits her story. Beautiful. Checkmate." He paused for effect, leaning forward on the back of Fuller's chair. "What do you know about this Winchell guy?" Brewster asked Fuller.

"Nothing," Fuller said. "He said he lives in Denver, but I don't even know if that is true."

Brewster walked to his desk. "Debbie," Brewster said into his intercom, "bring me the Denver phone book, would you?"

Within a few seconds Debbie appeared with the book, handed it to Brewster, and quietly excused herself. Brewster turned through the yellow pages until he found what he wanted. Then he turned to the white pages, scanned a page with his finger, and satisfied, closed the book and looked up at Fuller.

"Well?" Fuller said.

"Well, a Dan Winchell is listed as an attorney in Denver. Solo practice.

One of the few. Seems to be doing all right for himself. He lives on Fairfax Street. That's in Cherry Hills. High rent district."

"Now what?" Said Fuller.

"Let's see," said Brewster, "what we can find out about Mr. Winchell."

20

When David and Fuller left Brewster's office it was already three o'clock so they decided to stay in Gunther rather than make the 120 mile round trip to Henson. Brewster had said that he was going to see what he could find out about Winchell, and David and Fuller were anxious to hear what he had learned.

David had talked Fuller into eating at the A & W root beer drive-in, partly for nostalgia and partly so he could have a root beer float in a frosted mug. After supper, they got rooms at the Parkview Motel, and since it wasn't yet dark they went across the street and sat in the park, watching the sunset. There were only a few cars on the highway. On a low hill overlooking the town, someone had arranged white rocks to form a large *R*.

"What's the *R* for?" David asked.

"Rocky Mountain State College. It's there," he turned pointed behind the park. "The red brick buildings."

"Of course. I forgot about the college. Do you miss it?" David asked. "Teaching, I mean?"

"Not really," Fuller said flatly. "It was good for me then. But that was then. Another phase, as you would say." He smiled at David.

"I always thought I would like teaching. Provided I was independently wealthy."

"You'd need to be," Fuller agreed.

"I guess that's the wrong motive."

"Parts of teaching were good, especially in the beginning, when I was fresh from graduate school. Ideas. I was excited about ideas." He thought for a minute. "I remember this image that kept coming to me. I would be lecturing on something I was very enthusiastic about and I'd toss out these ideas. Like balloons. Blow up these idea balloons and tap them out over the

students." He mimed holding a balloon with one hand and tapping it with the other. "The balloon, a red one, would float out over the students, and one of them would reach up and grab it and tie it onto his head. Like this." Fuller tied an imaginary balloon on his head. "Then, I'd tap out another idea balloon, a blue one, and a student would grab it and tie it on. More ideas. More balloons. And when I had finished the lecture, I'd look out at the students. Some just sat there, blank-faced, bored. No balloons. But one or two students – only one or two – their faces beaming with excitement, sat there with all these balloons tied all over their heads." He made a wide circle over his head with his arms. "Balloons. That's what made teaching good. I'll miss those kids with the balloons."

While he was talking, the sun had gone down and a warm glow was all that was left of the day.

"You think you will ever go back to teaching?" David asked Fuller.

"Probably not." Fuller had never discussed "the accident" with David. He didn't even talk with his sister about it, although he knew sometimes she wanted to, to see if he was all right. David had never asked Fuller why he had left the college, and Fuller didn't see any need to bring it up. He just wanted to let it be. "Kinda' like you and medicine, I guess. It's somebody else's turn."

"Another phase," David said.

"Well," Fuller patted his thighs and stood up. "I guess this ol' fellow has had about enough for one day."

"Right," David said, taking Fuller's cue. "Me, too."

They walked back across the park toward the motel.

"Do you really think Winchell is lying to protect his mother?" David asked Winchellas they walked.

"You know," Fuller said, "after these past few days, I don't know what to think."

"She was pretty convincing, wasn't she?"

"Yeah," Fuller agreed. "And so was he."

Fuller's knock on the door woke David the next morning.

"Thought you might like some of these," Fuller said, handing him a paper sack. "Early Bird donuts. Best donuts on the Western Slope. I used to live on these babies. Donuts and coffee and cigarettes."

"Basic food groups," David smiled. He toasted Fuller with a donut and they ate breakfast in the room.

"Too cold to sit outside?" David asked.

"It is for me. The sun's up, but it's cold. It's only half past seven."

"Should we check out?" David asked.

"Might as well. If we're lucky, Brewster will have something to tell us this morning."

The office of the motel was about the same size as one of the guest rooms. A bell on the door tinkled when they entered. Behind the counter, through an open door, David and Fuller could see into the kitchen of the manager's apartment. Beside the counter was a postcard rack and a card of little aromatic Christmas trees, guaranteed to give your car the "smell of the Rockies." They told the manager that everything was fine when he asked, and David bought a tree for Fuller's jeep.

The two men left the motel office and walked along the broad main street talking. It was still but cool enough to make a jacket feel comfortable. Only a few pickups were on the street. Pickups wake up earlier than cars, David thought.

"It's all so confusing," David said as they walked. "Do you think Mrs. Winchell really made all that up about Hawthorne and the Mexicans?"

"I don't know," Fuller said. "It's hard to figure, isn't it? Maybe she really believes it. Maybe she is just a kooky old lady like Brewster says."

"She did seem a little different, now that I think about it," said David. "But why would she tell us all that. Doesn't that seem strange? I mean, it was all so private and personal."

"All of it seems a little strange to me."

"Maybe we were the only ones who had ever asked her about it." David said. "Maybe we flattered her. Neurotic people do tend to be self-centered. In their own world. Everything revolves around them. Especially if they are psychotic. They have trouble distinguishing between reality and imagination."

"Maybe she is just lonesome," said Fuller. They had stopped and stood talking in the sun in front of an old stucco building. It was one story and had full glass windows across the front. It looked like a converted shop or grocery store. While they looked at the store, a disinterested man with a white beard and matching hair turned the sign hanging in the door from "Closed" to "Open," then disappeared.

"Look at this stuff," David said, walking to the window.

"The Jackalope Shop," Fuller announced, joining him at the window. "Need a new buffalo robe? Or maybe a cow skull or two?"

Through the window David could see that the store was filled with a melange of rusted tools, wagon wheels, merry-go-round animals, saddles, faded blankets, animal skin rugs, an old gasoline pump, metal Coke signs, lamps, thermometers, clocks, hat racks with and without hats. Every inch of wall space was covered with animal heads, not only elk and deer and bear, but also antelope, zebra, a water buffalo. On a table at the rear of the room a full-sized mountain lion, yellow-eyed, snarled silently. Curlicues of sticky flypaper hung from the ceiling.

"You can get just about anything you need in there," Fuller said. "You should see this place in tourist season. He must make a fortune on this stuff."

"I'd love to have one of those bear rugs," said David. "But it would have to be one without a head. I couldn't deal with it looking at me all the time."

"He's got 'em," Fuller pointed out. There were several hanging on the wall.

"Well, actually," David admitted, " I never could buy one. I couldn't contribute to the market."

"But they're already dead," Fuller said.

"Well, someone would have to kill another bear to replace that one. I can't see killing a bear. I wouldn't want to be responsible for that."

"You know how they do it, don't you? How they hunt bears?" Fuller asked.

"I'm not sure I want to know."

"They hunt them from a stand in a tree. They bait them with Twinkies."

"I was afraid it was something like that."

"Maybe you could inherit a bear rug," Fuller joked.

"Or maybe find a bear that died of a heart attack."

"If this store is open, it must be about nine o'clock," said Fuller. "You don't have a watch, do you?"

"No," said David. "When I learned that the Navajos have no word in their language for time, I put it up."

"Good idea," said Fuller. "Let's go see if Brewster is in yet."

Debbie showed them into Brewster's office and explained that he would be

right in. David walked to the window, looked out at the street, beyond to the river, and the mountains. Pretty nice view for an office, David thought. He returned and sat in a chair next to Fuller. The walls of Brewster's office were covered with crowded bookshelves. Manila folders and papers were stacked on his desk and on the floor around it. It looked like a graduate student's room.

"You're gonna love this," Brewster said as he strode in. He was carrying more folders and a styrofoam coffee cup. He looked at the desk, then put the folders on the window sill with several others and turned to the men. "Want some coffee?" he said.

"No, thanks," said Fuller and David.

Brewster sat heavily in his chair and propped his black five-stitch boots on the corner of the desk. "Well," he began, catching his breath, "I called a friend in Denver. This Winchell is quite a guy. Stanford Law School, Class of 1961. Top ten percent of his class. Moved to Denver shortly after that and went into practice for himself. Apparently made his money in real estate. Anyway, he's loaded. He has mostly small clients, small developers and land dealers. Some independent oil operators. But he does have one big client." Brewster put his hands behind his head. "He's on retainer to Ardco. Ever heard of them?"

"No," said Fuller.

"Big California energy company. Oil. Oil shale. Natural gas. Pipelines. Big time. Winchell is their man in Denver."

"And," said Fuller when Brewster paused.

"And," Brewster said, swinging his feet onto the floor, leaning over his desk on his crossed forearms, "here's the zinger. Guess who owns Ardco?" Brewster smiled mischievously.

"I give up," Fuller said.

"The Hawthorne Family Trust," Brewster said in his best theatrical baritone.

"I'll be damned," David breathed.

"Idn't that something?" Brewster asked rhetorically. "Some things, the more you stir it, the worse it smells."

"The Hawthorne Family Trust," Fuller repeated.

"You've got it," Brewster said sitting back.

"So that's why he gave us the business about his mother," Fuller said. "He wasn't protecting his mother. He was protecting the Hawthornes."

"What else could he do?" Brewster said, shrugging his shoulders, palms up.

"Hey!" David said. "I just remembered something. When Winchell called me, he said he had gotten my number from the lady in the store in Cimarron. I never gave my number to that lady. You gave her your number," he said to Fuller. "I gave my number to the guy at the store in Moro!"

"I don't believe I would poke those guys with a sharp stick," said Brewster. "They are capable of causing you a whole lot of trouble."

"What about murder," Fuller said. "Would they have someone murdered to shut them up?"

"Murder is a big word," said Brewster.

21

"You're pretty sure the Hawthornes had Buster killed, aren't you?" David said to Fuller as they drove back to Henson.

"And Walker," said Fuller.

"They thought Buster might shoot his mouth off?"

"And they wanted to get the Cordovas' attention, too," Fuller added.

They drove several more miles in silence.

"What are you thinking?" David asked finally.

"Well," Fuller said," I'm thinking that I guess I won't be writing any book about James Hawthorne having Bill Walker killed to cover up his busted expedition."

"That's what I was thinking, too. But there's still the work about the route Hawthorne took. The watercolors. That's too good to give up on."

"Oh, we should still do that. You're still in this with me, aren't you?"

"You know I'd love it."

"Good. Shake, pardner." They shook hands across the jeep seat.

David leaned back in his seat and closed his eyes. He felt elated and letdown at the same time. It was really generous of Fuller to share his project with him. He felt lucky. Susan would be proud.

"You know something?" Fuller said casually.

"What's that?" David said.

"I heard once that some modern day mountain men said that they know where Bill Walker's body is buried."

David sat up with a jerk and turned to look at Fuller.

"It's somewhere in New Mexico," Fuller continued. "They want to

dig it up and return it to Colorado." He looked at David, smiling. "Want to go see if we can find it? I mean, as soon as this is done?"

David smiled and leaned back against the seat, pulling his hat down over his eyes. "Why not," he said. "Maybe the bear claw will be there."

At the south end of town, Fuller turned right on Silver Street and parked in front of the post office.

"Let's see if anybody sent us any checks," Fuller joked.

"Or death threats."

Fuller returned to the car with a two-day-old copy of the Sunday *New York Times* and one envelope which he tossed across the seat to David as he got in.

"Know anybody in Moro?" Fuller asked with a grimace.

David took the envelope without responding, tore open the end and began reading to himself.

"It's from Father Gabriel. A priest in Moro." He looked up at Fuller. "He says he has something to show us. He thinks we might be interested. It has something to do with Bill Walker."

The two men sat for a moment without speaking, looking at each other across the car seat.

"You don't suppose...," Fuller began.

"He wants to see us at ten o'clock."

22

The adobe church sat among the trees and dirt streets, a part of the land itself, like the hills around the village, soft and round, the color of coffee with just the right amount of milk. David turned into the bare churchyard and parked at the back of the building.

"He said to come in the back door," David recited.

"That must be it."

The two men walked to the door and stood for an uncomfortable moment. David glanced at Fuller, then knocked on the heavy door.

"Good morning, gentlemen." The priest was a slight man with close-cropped black hair and blacker eyes. His gray Franciscan robe appeared to have been made for a larger man. "You must be David Walton," he said, extending a soft hand. "The description was accurate." He turned to Fuller. "And Jack Fuller?"

How did he know my name, Fuller thought?

"Please come in." The small room was warm and aromatic from the piñon fire that burned in the kiva fireplace in the corner. A wide shaft of sunlight, dancing with particles, streamed in through the window behind the bed brightening a rectangle of tile floor, a table and four plain chairs.

"Please," the priest said, indicating the chairs. He waited for David and Fuller to sit and then joined them.

"You were surprised to hear from me?" The priest asked, smiling.

"Very much so," David said.

"I know of your interest," the priest said, sliding a business card across the table to David. It was the card David had left with Virgil.

The priest turned to Fuller. "An interest you must also share?"

Fuller nodded.

"Dr. Fuller wrote a book about James Hawthorne," David said. "I sought him out to help me with some questions I had about Hawthorne's last expedition."

"And that's why you came to Moro?" The priest said to David.

"Yes," David said. "We are interested in why the expedition failed so miserably. Exactly which route they took into the mountains, where they foundered and who chose the route. Most of the leads we had followed were dead-ends. Papers and records missing. Since Hawthorne's guide was killed somewhere near here..." David hesitated, "by Indians, we thought maybe there were still stories in the area, people who may have been told stories..." David was reluctant to tell the priest what they had learned from Ruth Winchell.

"Wasn't Hawthorne in charge?" The priest asked with mock innocence.

"Good point," said Fuller.

"Why, exactly, is it important for you to know this?" The priest asked.

It was a question David had not anticipated and it embarrassed him. He and Fuller had never discussed the "why", only the "what". David looked at Fuller. "I..." he began hesitantly, "I have to admit, Father, I don't know exactly what makes it so compelling. I suppose it's a form of vicarious adventure in a way. I have a longing to know these men, somehow. There is, of course, the selfish satisfaction of coming to the truth. The satisfaction that a scientist might seek. But with history, there is another level to it. It's more than the discovery of facts. It's a sort of voyeurism. A sharing of secrets, feelings, fears, hopes. If I actually knew what they did, somehow see them doing it..." He paused. "I suppose what I really want to know is how they felt."

"What will you do with this information?" The priest asked. "Is that a fair question?"

David hesitated. He glanced at Fuller. This will ruin it all, he thought. "We wanted to write a book. We wanted to write a book about this expedition. I must admit, I didn't start with that in mind. In the beginning it was the mystery of it that fascinated me. Just learning what was known about it. Later, the possibility of discovering exactly what happened, the satisfaction of solving it has been even more exciting. Now, well..."

The priest leaned back in his chair. "I was born in Moro," he said

quietly. "Like my father and his father before him. Five generations since they came, or were sent from Santa Fe, as you may know," he said with an understanding smile. "The old ones were called convicts. But for many of them, their only crime was resisting the Spanish. Resistance to tyranny is bravery to some, a crime to others."

He paused, looked out the window for a moment, then continued. "There were, to be sure, some evil men whose greed within them was unopposed by conscience and restraint. Men who might have made the kind of evil bargain that you have no doubt heard of. Or you would have never come here, would you?"

Fuller and David exchanged glances.

The priest rose and walked to the fireplace and turned to face them. "It was a terrible thing that these men did. I cannot excuse that, but perhaps..." His eyes looked to the ceiling. "For them. For us. For our little family. They were godless men. But it is not only they who suffer. The sins of the father shall be visited on the children," he quoted.

"And in our little family here, we are the children of these men. We have borne their shame all this time. It is a shame that has hung over this village like a cold cloud."

He walked through the wide shaft of sunlight to the window and without turning to them, continued. "After your visit, I met with the people here. I told them of your interest in Hawthorne and what that might mean. I told them I thought the time had come to break the silence, end the conspiracy of silence, and once and for all throw off the weight of the depression that we have unnecessarily borne. That as much as we regret what happened, it was unreasonable to continue to feel guilt for something we had no part of, except lineage. That because we could not condone the acts of our ancestors does not mean that we could not be proud of ourselves. It is time, I said, and in the telling of it is our salvation."

The priest turned to face David and Fuller. "I asked them to go to their homes and think about what I had said. That I would not violate their conscience. That without their permission I would remain silent. But I urged them to put all of this behind us. Last week, just before I wrote to you, they came to me with their answer."

The priest walked to a closet and returned to the table with a brown paper package. "The story you have heard is true. The story has been

told to everyone in this village, even by his father. A man traveling through this country that spring was killed by men who lived near this village. While in Blanco they had been approached by a man who had just come from the mountains to the west. He told them that his companion had stolen money from him, silver coins, and that he was expected in the valley within a week. The man said he wanted his companion dead, and that if they killed him, they were welcome to have the money he carried. The man said that all he asked was, that as proof, the men were to take from his companion a bear claw he wore around his neck. He said someday he would come for it. He never came back for the claw. It was once in the village, but now it is gone."

David and Fuller exchanged glances.

"There is something else, however." The priest placed the package on the table and pushed it across to David."

"Go on. Open it," the priest said when David seemed hesitant.

David removed the paper wrapper. Inside was a small book, bound in dark leather, frayed and faded russet around the edges.

"As you will see," the priest continued, "this is a diary kept on the mountain expedition. It was with the money and other effects stolen from the murdered man we now know was Bill Walker. It is a fascinating little book, and will no doubt be of great interest to you and will no doubt answer all of your questions."

David touched the diary lightly without opening it.

"There is one thing, however. You must understand that this whole affair is a very unpleasant thing for these people. It is something that, having dealt with, they are very much now anxious to put behind them. Please examine it in here. In this room. Take as long as you like to satisfy yourselves and learn what you need to know. But I must tell you, you may take with you only what your memory can carry. When you have finished, the book must be destroyed. For them it is a symbol of something that is very unpleasant. That is their wish. I could promise them no less."

"But..." David began.

"Please," said the priest, his hand raised. "I have no choice."

"And if we decide not to look at it?" Fuller asked.

"That is your choice. But whatever your decision, I must destroy it

as I have been asked to do. I will leave you to yourselves." The priest walked to the door and left.

"Well" David said with a sigh. "Here's what we have been looking for. You up to this?"

"Never been more ready."

The paper backing cracked as David opened the cover. The blue-lined paper was water stained but the crude writing was legible.
He began to read.

WEDNESDAY NOV 22

raised camp aT 5 1/2 – cold sTill
sTill snowing on The mounTains
I wanT To go one way and
HawThorne will go anoTher
righT here our Troubles
will commence...